A Bathory Universe Novel

Knight OF THE *Hunted*
SPECIAL EDITION

Get bitten!

NSFW EDITION
THE BORN VAMPIRE SERIES BOOK ONE
ELIZABETH DUNLAP

INTRODUCTION

Warning: For Adult Audiences 18+.Language and actions may be deemed offensive to some. Sexually explicit content. M/F

OTHER BOOKS BY ELIZABETH DUNLAP

Born Vampire Series: Ya Edition (Completed)

Knight of the Hunted (1)

Child of the Outcast (2)

War of the Chosen (3)

Bite of the Fallen (4)

Rise of the Monsters (5)

Time of the Ancients (6)

Born Vampire Series: NSFW Edition (Completed)

Knight of the Hunted (1)

Child of the Outcast (2)

War of the Chosen (3)

Bite of the Fallen (4)

Rise of the Monsters (5)

Time of the Ancients (6)

Born Vampire Short Stories

Tales of the Favored: Arthur's Tale (3.5)

Affairs of the Immortal: The Sinful Affair (4.4)

Affairs of the Immortal: The Knight and Arthur Affair (4.5)

Affairs of the Immortal: The Valentine's Day Affair (6.5)

A Grumpy Fairy Tale Series

The Grumpy Fairy (1)

The Dragon Park (2)

Ecrivain Academy Series

Ecrivain (1)

Neck-Romancer Series

Neck-Romancer (1)

Neck-Rological (2)

Highborn Asylum Series

Freak: A Highborn Asylum Prequel

Stand-Alones

LAP Dogs (coming soon)

This is a work of fiction. Names, characters, places, and incidents either are the product of the author's imagination or are used fictitiously, and any resemblance to any persons, living or dead, business establishments, events, or locales is entirely coincidental.

Dedicated to the three women I send everything to.
I can always send you my crazy ideas, night or day, and you'll help
me out <3

1

A BLOODY TURNING

Upstate New York, 2017

I woke up to the scent of blood in my room. Blood and coffee. I opened my eyes and saw my companion sitting in my armchair, sipping a mug and playing a game on his phone. My cursory glance turned into a scowl when I noticed he was wearing a pair of Pokémon pajamas, and no shirt. Admittedly, Cameron was very attractive and had enough muscles to make any girl swoon. Not me, however, but I still enjoyed the view. He fiddled with his rusty red bleached hair as he concentrated on his game.

"What are you doing, Cameron? You know you're not supposed to be in here." Yawning, I stretched my arms above my head and pushed long black curls out of my face. My golden comforter crinkled when I slid off the bed and onto the soft vanilla carpet. He was lucky I'd worn pajamas. That would've been embarrassing.

"I was going about my merry business and heard you shouting in your sleep. When I walked in, you calmed down, so I stayed." He looked up from his game and gave me a half smile, his brown Japanese eyes showing sympathy. "Finneus. That's what you kept shouting."

My dream resurfaced in a cold flash. A memory from another life. One I'd tried hard to forget. "He was my friend when I was a girl. The humans killed him by burning his house down." I could still feel that moment like it had been yesterday. The raging heat of the flames. The screams as they turned to ash. I wrapped myself in my arms to try and shake away the memory and the icy sadness it brought. "It was a long time ago."

"Right," Cameron murmured gently. "So, was that five hundred or six hundred years ago?"

"Screw you, I'm not THAT old."

"Okay, old lady," he tossed, and looked back at his game. I was about to reprimand him, even though he was just messing with me, when a knock came at the front door of my suite. "That'll be Othello," Cameron groaned with annoyance. "That man is the definition of 'no means yes and yes means anal.' Like seriously." I slipped on a robe, shook a warning finger at Cameron, and walked into the living room. When I opened the Venetian front door, the stink of dead flowers smacked me in the face like bad breath. The head of my Order stood holding a gorgeous flower bouquet for me, the source of the disgusting smell.

"Good morning, Lisbeth," Othello said brightly, a smile on his gaunt face. I'm sure when he was younger he was quite handsome, but at that moment he looked like he'd walked straight out of a Dracula novel. Not the kind of guy you'd want to wake up to, I can tell you that. I took the bouquet from him and heard Cameron leaving my bedroom. Othello almost showed displeasure when he noticed my companion coming from my room, but he hid it well. "It's almost time for the meeting. It'll be in the drawing-room. The bigger one." He waited for me to respond, maybe say thank you for the flowers, but I remained silent. As the head of my order, he had the power to choose any of us as his mate, but he'd set his eyes on me.

Even though I'd told him to back off several times, he still came by every day with flowers so he could compliment my hair and scowl at my companion. It's not like I had sex with Cameron. That didn't happen between a vampire and their companion. He seemed convinced naked things would happen eventually. Boys fall for girls, you know.

"I'll be down directly," I told Othello and promptly shut the door in his gaunt white face. "God fucking, ugh, he is the worst."

I turned to one of my display tables where I kept my vases, Cameron was sitting on one of my gaudy Victorian couches, still playing his game, but wearing a shirt this time and hiding all those muscles of his. "Fucking him would be the grossest thing ever," he muttered in Japanese. I giggled and replaced the poppy bouquet from yesterday with today's roses. I sprayed the flowers with some essential oil so the disgusting scent would go away before I got back.

On a normal morning, I would've drunk from Cameron and then we would go down for breakfast. Today wasn't normal. Today was the most important day of the year. I went back to my room, changed into a black and white dress, and ran a brush through my black curls until they looked presentable. When I returned to the living room, Cameron was waiting for me, also changed.

"Like what you see?" Cameron offered, smirking at me. I realized I'd been standing there for a few minutes, staring at his outfit.

"If you ever see me naked, you'll know I do." He rolled his eyes and we both started towards the door.

"Me first, old lady." Instead of letting him pass, I picked him up and walked out into the hall, then deposited him on the thick red carpet. "Ugh. I hate when you do that," he groaned. "Makes me feel so unmanly."

I stuck my tongue out at him. "You know you love me."

He sighed and smiled at me. "And to think, ten years ago you didn't know how to be sarcastic. Now it's all I hear."

"God forgive him because he knew not what he was doing," I joked, and we walked down the hallway. At the stairs, Cameron and I parted ways. He went to the kitchen, and I made my way down the long ground floor hallway to the drawing-room. The bigger one. It was a large dark green

4

room with a big ass window that let in enough sunlight to chase away any memory of darkness. A nice fuck you to the turned vampires, in my opinion. The sunlight meant they couldn't be in this room without one of us pulling the curtains closed.

My work partner and best friend, Olivier, was waiting for me. We educated the turned vampires together. Unlike most Born vampires, she was of African descent, and her dark skin looked like a rare diamond amongst all the paleness. Her style of dress was the a-typical mermaid black lace confections, a silent joke against stereotypes that she adamantly denied.

I walked up to her and tugged on one of her Steampunk style dreads. "I vant to suck your blood," I whispered, giving her my best Dracula impression.

She looked up and narrowed her eyes at me. "Girl, are you making fun of my dress?"

I tried to look innocent. "Of course not."

She scowled, jokingly, then smiled at me. "Speaking of Dracula, did you finally submit to his will after he gave you roses?" She could smell the bouquet from Othello on my skin.

"Almost, but the scent of dead flowers was a real turn off." Not that I'd *been* turned on, mind you.

"You'd think he'd understand a no by now," she commented, flipping through a folder on the table. "Your ass is just too sexy. He can't help himself."

"Cute," I said, bumping her with my hip playfully. Before I

could say more, the person in question walked over to us. We straightened up and pretended to be occupied.

He was all business this time, though he did give me looks that had that 'I like working with you' vibe. Gag. "Alright, ladies. They're coming in now. Remember that flashing your fangs or making scary faces is NOT funny. The humans need to think we're civilized." He handed me a clipboard with names on it and walked past us over to one of the doors.

"Did you hear that, Lisbeth? Be civilized." Olivier playfully smacked my arm. Othello gave us the same warning every time, but to be fair we hadn't played a joke on anyone in several decades.

"Civilized, my ass," I told her, sticking my tongue out.

Othello clapped his hands to get us to zip it and opened the huge door to the adjoining sitting room. Inside the sitting room was a group of humans who had been selected and prepared for today. The day they would become the turned.

"Welcome, my friends," Othello said brightly, holding his arms out. "Please come into the drawing-room." They all got up and followed Othello back to where we stood. "I won't make you suffer with anticipation, so we shall journey below to the dormitory and begin."

One of the humans apparently hadn't been paying attention, because why the fuck would he, and he brought his hand up to ask a question. "Why is it in the basement?" the human male asked.

Othello smiled at the human like he was struggling to be patient. *Listen here, bitch.* "Once you join the turned, the sun will burn your skin and turn you to ash." As if on cue, the humans looked at the enormous window behind me. The warmth of the sun was pouring through the paned glass onto my arms and back. Damn, it felt nice, like a soft comfy blanket. "This is your last chance to feel the sunlight," Othello warned them. "You will never walk outside in the sun again." We waited, but none of the humans walked over to the window to soak in the sun. They'd already accepted their new life.

That made my job easier, thank god.

Olivier picked up the enormous ice chest filled with bagged blood and followed me to the basement door. The humans started a line behind us, and we all started walking down the darkened hallway that led downstairs.

"Hey," one of the humans whispered, trying to catch up with me. I kept walking but turned my head to look at him. He was an older man and had a kind face. "What's in the ice chest?"

Olivier made a frustrated noise and grumbled in a pitch only I could hear, "Don't fucking humans ever pay the fuck attention?" A mystery for all the ages.

Still, I smiled at the man, channeling all the patience I knew I had. "It's blood. All part of the process."

We reached the doors to the basement staircase and the human male stood very close to me as the group stopped. *Back that ass up, son.* "I thought we'd be given a feeder."

7

This bitch.

"Companion," I corrected with a twinge of annoyance. Calling our companions feeders was extremely rude. A feeder was a hit and run drink, like a one-night stand, and we didn't treat humans that way. Making them our companions gave them anything they needed in return for their service. It was only polite. "You won't be given a *companion* for the first month, not until you've learned to control your thirst." I glanced at Olivier, and with a nod, I opened the doors and let the humans in.

At the bottom of the stairs was the turned vampire dormitory. There were rows of coffins, each with a small nightstand and dresser next to it. The coffins weren't necessary, it was just a bit of vampire humor, like Olivier's wardrobe. You couldn't say we didn't have a sense of humor.

There was no electricity in this room, and dozens of candles lit our way across the stone floor to the rest of my Order, all Born vampires. They stood in the center of the chamber, waiting for us to reach them. The younger vampires would turn at least one human. The older vampires, myself included, would turn however many we needed to. I glanced at my clipboard and called out all the humans' names and which vampire was to turn them. Olivier and I had three humans, and Othello had four.

Then it began.

The room started to stink of fear. No matter how much preparation the humans had had, seeing us drop our fangs brought out their primal fear, and it wasn't surprising. They

8

were our prey and had been for thousands of years. Only within the last few centuries had we become a civilized species. Well, most of us. Some of us still liked to fuck shit up, but we dealt with them accordingly.

The younger Born drank from their assigned human, just a pint or so. My three humans stood nearby, one of them the human male that had spoken to me. Their faces paled in fear when I dropped my fangs and leaned into the first human's neck. The woman's blood filled my mouth, and my entire body seemed to breathe a sigh of relief. Fuck, I hadn't noticed my hunger until I was already drinking. I was careful to not drink too much from them, not to spare them the effects of blood loss, but so I didn't over drink. I took only a mouthful from each one.

When every human had been fed from, we tore into our wrists and pressed it to their mouths. The humans were disgusted at the taste of our blood. That would soon change.

As soon as our blood hit their stomachs, the process began. They screamed in white-hot agony and fell to the ground, their bodies no longer willing to support their weight. We backed away as they writhed on the floor, wracked with pain. The vampire blood worked its way through their systems quickly, but Olivier still had enough time to distribute a bag of blood to every Born vampire. I balanced three of the bags in my arms, and we all waited for the writhing and screaming to stop.

The humans soon grew still. They were now technically dead, for the moment. Their bodies had changed. All imperfections were gone. Those that had been old were now young. The overweight had shed every extra pound, and their once pink skin was now pale. They were beautiful in death.

Collectively, they all came back to life, gasping in a breath, and opened their eyes.

They were no longer humans.

They had become the turned.

2

POWDERED CONFECTIONS

*A*s soon as the turned opened their eyes, their thirst stirred in a blinding flash. I handed my three their bags of blood, and they tore into the plastic with their new fangs. Blood spilled, half in their mouths and half on their clothes. One bag was enough to keep them from becoming drones, the mindless servants we can create but are forbidden to. A disappointing rule, because everyone wants fucking servants, amirite? Kidding.

Now the next stage began: the turned would be denied blood until they could control themselves. We overpowered them and locked one in each of the coffins in the room.

Then the real screams began.

The screams during the turning were bad enough, but the screams during this process were maddening. Imagine the sound of someone seeing their family murdered in front of them while being burned with acid and having their hair pulled out. Not only were the screams ones of physical pain, they were filled with emotional agony. It was fucking disconcerting on every level, and I wanted to turn my goddamn ears off. We all had the same look. We were used to this. We did it every year. But the screams. The shouting, ranting, and clawing. God, I could never get used to them. It would be days before the turned had learned control. The screaming would continue until tomorrow, at the earliest, and only if we were lucky.

Unable to take it anymore, I excused myself, along with a few others who had things to do. Olivier walked beside me until I reached the kitchen cafeteria room. The door opened to the clean white walls and stainless steel appliances, the only room of our home that was completely upgraded and up to date. Cameron stood in the cooking section, eating an orange. He smiled tentatively at me when we approached. The screams still floated up to us, muffled, but there. He couldn't hear them as well as we could, but the look on his face said he could hear them well enough.

"What was it like?" he asked. We both froze and stared at him. He'd never asked that before, not in the ten years he'd been here.

"You want to know about the turning?" I asked him in disbelief, leaning against the polished metal door of one of the fridges.

He waved his hand at me in dismissal. "No, not that. I

mean before there was bagged blood. Before you had rules about turning."

Olivier quirked an eyebrow at him. "Son, you really don't want to know our history."

He bit into his orange and stared at her, more serious than I'd ever seen him. "I asked," he said firmly. "I want to know."

Olivier leaned one hip against the dark countertops. "You know how they say history is written by the victors? Well, our phrase is: history is written by the humans. And humans can be…persuaded…to forget what really happened."

"Shit. You are NOT talking mind control." He looked over at me. "Is she talking mind control? Like, I'd rather not pay my tab tonight thank you, or you will give me your ticket to see Bob Marley?"

I scrunched up my mouth, not wanting to answer. Everyone has their illicit topics. "It's technically forbidden now. But yes, we can do it." Cameron's mouth popped open in shock. I couldn't tell if he was joking or being serious. "It's only possible if you feed multiple times a day, and even then, you have to be a few hundred years old to boot."

"Give me an example," he said, turning his body so he could see both of us. "Something in history that was fucked with."

Olivier pulled herself onto the black marble countertop and inspected her long nails. "You've heard of the Black Plague? The sweating sickness?" He nodded, so she grinned widely, showing her fangs. "Vampires."

Cameron's mouth popped back open. "You're fucking joking."

I shook my head and picked up an apple from the fruit basket on the expensive marble countertop that Olivier shouldn't be sitting on. "Almost every plague was an altered event that involved vampires. Maybe there was an actual sickness that had spread. It was never to the degree of a plague though. The death tolls rose because of us."

"That's what happens when you let turned ass loose before they've learned control," said Olivier in a reproaching tone. "And even though we're born with control, the Born have been known to break the rules now and then. There was one Born vampire that changed hundreds of humans in an instant. His ass bit hundreds across a city over several months and dropped his blood in their water supply. Then they turned, without any supervision or training. It was a goddamn massacre waiting to happen." I scraped at my apple's peel and studied the floor. The past had its ghosts, that much was certain.

Cameron clicked his tongue, making me look up. "You act so damned repulsed by murder. You can't tell me neither of you has ever killed before." I opened my mouth, then closed it, and continued running my nails against the apple in my hand. I felt some peel come off.

"There's a difference between killing to feed and killing just to kill," I said quietly.

Olivier didn't feel as bad as I did about that part of our

past. "We did what we had to. To protect the masses, and to survive. Don't fault us for that."

"That's just it," he said, looking down. "I'm not sure I do, to tell you the truth. I guess that's what bothers me." He tossed his orange peel into the trash bin and left the room.

Olivier watched him go then glanced back at me. "What was all that shit about? He's never been interested in us before." I shrugged. In the past decade, he'd never asked me about my life before him beyond the occasional crack at our decor. He'd always given me the impression he would be gone as soon as his time was up. There was a first time for everything, I suppose.

A bloodcurdling scream came from the basement, startling me.

"Shit," I swore under my breath. Several of the turned were now wailing at the top of their lungs, and it was only going to get worse. I couldn't handle this crap today. I needed to get out.

After a quick trip upstairs to grab my purse, I trekked down to the turned dormitory and walked past the screaming coffins. Not that I wanted to go that way, but it's the only route, unfortunately. Whoever designed this castle should be shot, seriously. The underground garage was through a side door between two coffins. I had the status to hire a driver and be driven wherever I wanted to go, but I preferred to drive myself. My car was pretty and black, and got all the stares in town. I suspected it was expensive, but I had no idea. A car junkie I was not.

Our large castle was a few minutes outside of the nearest town and it didn't take me long to drive there. I parked in front of one of the bookstores I frequented and went inside. The smell of books hit me like a relaxing wave and I sighed in relief. Getting lost in the shelves would calm me down enough to face more screaming. Just as I'd found a section to peruse, I felt a breeze and smelled lilac.

Balthazar.

I turned to see my oldest friend, an Incubus. He was wearing a handsome dark blue suit, and his lengthy black hair hung in slight waves. He leaned on his cane and gave me the grin I'd seen from birth. The grin that made human women melt into puddles and beg to be seduced by him.

Gods above, he was the sexiest thing I'd ever seen.

"Hello, Balthy," I said with a smile, trying to calm my slowly heating body. "You can stop giving me the Incubus smolder. It's not appropriate to turn your friends on in public."

"Hmm... remember what I said I'd do if you called me Balthy again...." He wiggled his eyebrows and reached a hand out to me to extract his punishment.

My smile fell and I gave him a stern glare. "Don't make me slap you." He laughed and used his hand to bring me closer for a peck on the cheek.

Balthazar had appeared for the first time when I was a young child. He said he was a friend of my mother's, a woman I had never known, and he was going to watch over me. His presence in my life was unheard of. The Bicus,

Incubi and Succubi, never had anything to do with vampires and Lycans beyond creating us, which was now banned for an unknown reason. Everyone knew about Balthazar, but it was bizarre to the other Born that he liked to visit me. He'd always been around, popping in every so often, and he usually seemed genuinely interested in me and what I was doing. Though sometimes he would get distracted by a human female, and then it was like I didn't exist.

Like right then, for instance.

He'd been smiling at me, studying my face, when he glanced behind me and suddenly saw prey. I could see the world melt away around him, and all that mattered was the human female he'd spotted. I turned to look at her. She was a little mousy thing, clearly quite pretty under her oversized glasses, but she had no confidence and dressed badly. Underneath the droopy skirt she was wearing, her ass was nice and round. Her golden hair was in a tight bun, the kind men fantasized about pulling the pins out of to see how soft it was as they push her body against the bookshelves. And her lips were so soft and full, you could only guess what kind of sounds would come out of them if you fucked her in the bookstore bathroom. I bet she'd moan like a bitch in heat if you touched her in the right places.

She was an Incubus's wet dream. She was any man's wet dream. Hell, even I was fantasizing about her. I hadn't had a lover in many years, man or woman. A tryst in the shadows didn't sound like a bad idea, especially with her.

Beside me, Balthazar was also fantasizing about the

woman it seemed, and fingernails had started to grow into long claws, the Bicus equivalent of an erection. Rest assured, he had one of those too.

I punched his arm.

He yelped, and his fingernails retracted as he reached up to rub where I'd hit him. I held my fist out, ready to smack his arm again, but the girl picked up a romance novel with a barely dressed sensual couple on the front, and left. He sighed and looked back at me while adjusting his tie and slicking back his hair.

"Thanks for that. I was two seconds away from breaking the rules and tearing her clothes off right here to fuck her against the stacks."

"I was two seconds away from fighting you for that right, but I know I'd lose." I was a sex goddess, for certain, but he was sex itself. I'd never get chicks with him here. "On the subject, why is banging humans and creating more children forbidden now? You guys have been doing that for thousands of years, and then a few hundred years ago, suddenly, no more sex. Thoughts?"

He shrugged, being his evasive self. Not that I hadn't been asking for four hundred years. I'm very persistent. "Lisbeth, my sweet. What shall we do today? I'm up for... anything." He fluttered his eyelashes at me. Fuuck. I hated it when he did that. I could only be so turned on.

"Do I have to hit you again?"

He clicked his tongue and poked me with his cane.

"Come. I require sustenance in the form of powdered doughnuts. Only confections can remove thoughts of sex."

I picked up a few books I thought looked interesting, including a copy of the sexy book Miss Plump Lips had bought. I paid for them and we left the store. It was unclear to me if Balthazar even needed food, but he usually ate with me whenever he came to visit. As he said, it was the only thing that made him stop focusing on sex. The human women that passed us felt his presence like a sex beacon, each one doing a double take or stopping in their tracks to stare. The smell of their arousal started to fill the air from his aura. It took focus for me to not be affected by him. Maybe one day I wouldn't care, and I'd let that aura swallow me whole.

Every woman might've been gaping at him, but he continued walking beside me as if he didn't notice. When it was clear he wasn't going to talk to them, the humans started glaring at me, so I pulled a book out of my bag and pretended to be absorbed in it. Ohh. A sex scene.

"Great. Just what I need, to be more turned on." I started putting it back into my bag when Balthazar took it from me.

"What in God's name are you reading?" He started to chuckle as he flipped through the pages. "They call this making love? Pssh. I'm much better." I rolled my eyes.

We arrived at the tea café and walked inside. I took in the beautiful British design the café had as we waited to be seated. The air smelled like strawberry jam and cream with a hint of mint tea leaves. It was the main reason I liked the place. We were led to a table and Balthazar sat down across from me, still reading. The waiter walked up, a handsome male, who obviously preferred the company of men, judging by the once-over he was giving Balthazar. Balthazar was holding the book very close to his face so I couldn't tell if he noticed the waiter checking him out or not. I ordered doughnuts with raspberry tea and the waiter left.

Balthazar peeked out from the paperback. "Is he gone?" I nodded, so he exhaled and set the book down. "I don't have a problem with an attractive man, I just can't impregnate one, so what's the point." I stifled a laugh in my hand because he said it so matter of fact-ly. Balthazar took my other hand when he noticed the waiter coming back with our tea. He left again, taking the hint with a slight pout.

I took my hand back and poured us tea from the flowery china teapot. "Just be glad he's not a woman. Do you seriously not notice what happens when you're around humans?"

He sighed and rolled his eyes. "Of course I notice, my love. You don't know how many times I've wished I could turn my damned aura off. But no. They're my prey. As if I NEED an aura when my literal purpose is to lure them in with the promise of passion." Balthazar sipped his tea after I'd finished adding sugar and milk to it. "The turning was today," he stated, carefully watching my face.

My back automatically stiffened, but I tried to be cavalier about it. "You'd think I'd be used to it by now," I said disarmingly. But the screams. Oh, those terrible screams.

"Yes. They are quite horrid," Balthazar remarked quietly, and I realized I'd spoken out loud. "They will be over soon. And then you'll be too busy to see me. Maybe I'll have to have that gorgeous woman to myself if you don't visit."

We playfully argued over that for a few minutes, and then we chatted about nothing and everything for hours, sipping fruit-flavored tea and eating powdery desserts. Being with Balthazar was nice. He grounded me in a way my other friends couldn't. He never reproached me, no matter what I discussed with him, and he never treated me like I was dense when I asked a simple question.

The only thing I was never allowed to ask him about was my mother and grandmother. I knew he knew them, only because one time during the French Revolution he was drunk on whatever can actually get an Incubus drunk, and he kept talking about how much he missed my grandmother and how much I looked like her. As far as I could find out, no one else knew who my mother and grandmother were. My father was a bigger mystery, one Balthazar didn't even know. A mystery I'd convinced myself held no interest to me.

When my stomach had reached its limit, in addition to the blood I'd drunk earlier, we left the tea shop and strolled through a park nearby, recounting old memories in soft tones that the humans wouldn't hear. I wasn't sure what the response would be if they overheard Balthazar recalling Nefertiti's wardrobe choices.

When morning turned into afternoon, my mobile buzzed signaling a text from Olivier.

Get your white ass home. We have things to do.

As soon as I'd finished reading it, I felt a flutter of wind and my walking companion was no longer there. Balthazar enjoyed showing off his incorporeal abilities by appearing and disappearing at will. And that included several occasions when he was suddenly not there as the conversation got boring. God damn it. I'd have to walk back alone. I swore and cursed him under my breath for leaving me miles away from my car without someone to talk to as I walked back. By the time I returned to my car, I was half angry at the state of my hair from the wind blowing it, and half at the fact that the trip could've taken only a few minutes if I had used my true speed. I knew better than to zip across a human walk-way. That didn't mean I wasn't tempted.

I started driving back home, but I felt itchy to move my muscles. Pulling over, I parked my car on the side of the deserted road and got out. I put my hair back into a ponytail and started running down the street at top speed. Trees became a blur, and the smell of everything I was passing hit me all at once. Rain puddles, pine trees, asphalt, and the lingering scent of human, a companion from our house if I was correct.

My ears could pick up animals miles away; rabbits, mice, and the occasional big game. The sharpness in senses I was feeling only happened when I ran. My brain was processing everything quickly, mapping out in my head what my preda-tory instincts needed in case I wanted to hunt. The thought of hunting made me slow down.

There was no denying what I was. I had never been ashamed of being a Born vampire. It was only my centuries of experience that made killing humans so utterly abhorrent to me. They were frail. Their lives ended. One mistake, one decision could end them forever. And then your friend was never there again. Lives were too precious for that.

"Nice legs, Forest Gump."

I looked up and realized I'd already reached the front gate of my home. Cameron stood in the front lawn peering over the tall stone fence with a smirk on his face. I hoped for his sake he wasn't trampling the hedges.

"I felt like running," I said out loud, even though he hadn't asked me anything about what I was doing.

"I can see that," he replied. "And your car is..." I pointed behind me and winced when he instantly looked murderous. "You left. Your sports car. ON THE FUCKING HIGHWAY??"

I winced again and tried to defend myself. "It's not like people drive out here, seriously. I wouldn't be running if they were." I vaguely wondered why I was making excuses to someone less than a fourth my age, but Cameron's glare made me feel like a fledgling again.

"Go the hell back. Pick your damn car up. Carry it home. If there's a single scratch, I will force you to listen to Justin Beaver."

"Who?" I asked dumbly.

"MARCH!"

I grumbled and turned around, then went into a light

sprint back to my car. Funny how just this morning, I was the bossy older person in this relationship. I didn't, in fact, pick up my car and carry it back. I might be able to run fast enough so a human couldn't see me, but there was no way I could hide carrying a car down the road.

As soon as I got back and parked in the underground garage, Cameron was there swinging around a yo-yo, waiting for me. He walked over, swinging his yo-yo to narrowly miss my face (show off), and inspected my car. "Good girl. You pass." I flipped him off.

Our smiles faded when we opened the door leading to the turned dormitory. The screams had died down a little; they'd lost that agonizing tone that made them so hard to listen to. The room felt cold and dreary, and the coffins didn't help the atmosphere feel less like a death chamber. Cameron's fingers started twitching so he stuffed his hands in his pockets.

In the center of the room stood creepy face Othello, looking over some paperwork with one of the Born that handled the companion system. A few bigger vampires stood guard among the coffins, making sure the turned didn't escape. They were locked in, of course, but sometimes a strong one broke out and had to be dealt with. And by dealt with, I mean we beat their ass and put them back in.

"Ah, there you are," Othello said as we approached, handing off the papers in his hand, and motioned for the companion supervisor to leave. The other vampire winked at Cameron as she passed. I growled a warning to her to keep her hands to herself. Cameron started coughing into his hand, hiding a laugh. "They should be ready in the morning," Othello told us, like the turned were baked chickens in the oven. Though it was kind of true, I suppose. He gave me a once-over, stopping at my breasts for an appreciative look, and that was my cue to leave, before I tore his head off. I grabbed Cameron's elbow and we left the basement.

When we entered the larger drawing-room, Olivier was lounging on a divan with a binder in her hands that had a cartoon vampire on the cover. Her companion, Renard, sat next to her and his hand drew lazy circles on her arm, the other held a goblet of wine. He was a devoted Frenchman, very sexy, and liked to sass his Lady as much as possible. This was his third tenure with her. Age had only made him more handsome. Romantic relationships between vampires and humans were forbidden, but that didn't stop any of us from looking the other way when these two started flirting. I'll admit, I wanted them to hook up. A stolen kiss, a tryst in the woods. I'd never tell anyone.

Renard jumped up and tipped his faded top hat to me, exposing his buzzed red hair. "*Ah, ma belle mademoiselle*[1]!" he said brightly with a twist of his barbell mustache. "Do not worry, *ma Cherie*[2]," he added, turning to Olivier who was ignoring him. "There is no one as *charmante*[3] as you."

"Ass," she muttered in French before calling him stupid, and a few other things that weren't so *charmante* of her. Renard dropped his outspread arms and gave her the stink eye. She smirked, still focused on her binder.

And that's what I meant by flirting.

Renard rolled his eyes and sat back down to drink from his chalice. "The screams have gotten better. *Mon dieu*[4]. That is a relief on my ears." He'd been here long enough to have a vampire-like attitude about it, but I could still see circles under his eyes. He downed his wine in one long gulp.

Olivier closed her vampire binder and sighed. "I can't wait until tomorrow when we can start getting some fucking work done. God, I hate sitting around." Before she came here, she had been one of the Hunters, the vampire police. They traveled in a small group, hunting down those of us that broke the law. The vampire law, I might add, not human law. We didn't abide by their rules. A Hunter's job never ended, they were always pursuing a subject. Always. I didn't know why Olivier decided to leave them and come here, and I knew better than to ask.

She wasn't the only one looking forward to tomorrow when the screams would stop and the work began.

3

BACON, BACON, BACON

*S*leeping didn't come easily that night. Olivier and I had spent the rest of the day going over paperwork. Cameron went to his room as soon as we finished dinner, leaving me by myself in the large castle. After all my work was done, I went to my room and changed into a nightgown, but after an hour of lying in bed, I was still wide-awake. I put on a kimono robe and went downstairs to the library. Maybe I'd read more of that sexy book and do a little rub a dub dub.

The large library was part of the turned portion of the castle. Red carpet, red walls, electric candelabras instead of normal lighting, and heavy curtains at the windows that could be drawn during the day. The Born rooms were bright with large windows and no curtains. This was, after all, our home. After the turned were trained, they would all leave and be reassigned to another Order. We were the oldest group of vampires and maintained our purity. The turned were not allowed to have a permanent residence here. It was a bit snobby, but who was I to scoff at tradition?

Waiting for me in the library was a sleeping figure on one of the ornate sofas. I smelled wine and brandy. Moving closer, I saw Renard's sleeping face. His snores made his barbell mustache flutter. A large and mostly empty bottle of brandy lay atop a stack of books on the floor in front of him. I reached down and picked it up, my eyes searching the red carpet for the lid.

"*Amore...mi amore*[1]," Renard muttered in his sleep. He suddenly came awake when I reached beside him to retrieve the brandy lid. "*Ah, belle Lisbeth.*" He sat up and scrubbed a hand down his face to scratch at his red stubble.

"Did Olivier kick you out again?" I asked him, only half serious. She'd only done so once in their thirty years together. He dared to make a joke about her vampire mermaid dresses. Or maybe they'd finally made love and she regretted it. Who knew.

Renard's violet eyes caught the moonlight, a shade lighter than my own purple eyes. It seemed as if all our companions had some exotic quality, like how humans kept exotic pets. Bad analogy. "*Non.* I needed to drown the damn noise." The screams were still going on downstairs, and all the tuning out in the world couldn't make me not hear it. The turned were close to being ready, and in a last push, they'd gotten louder hoping we'd let them out. It wouldn't work.

Renard got up and gently took the bottle from my hand, then leaned down to my face and kissed my cheek. "Back to my Lady. *Bon chance*[2]." He sauntered out, grabbing onto something for balance a few times. I sat on the sofa he'd been sleeping on and plopped my head down to the headrest.

My eyes closed. Instantly, I felt someone push a cup of coffee in my face. I sat up quickly, startled, and saw Cameron in front of me, laughing. It was morning already, the sun beat into the red room without the curtains to block it. I'd fallen asleep without even noticing. I started adjusting my kimono robe and noticed Cameron had brought me a dress with shoes that matched it. He turned his back so I could change.

"Thanks," I said to Cameron when I was done. He turned and handed me my mug of coffee. We sipped in awkward silence, both unconsciously testing to hear if the screams had stopped. I counted two individual screams from the dormitory, the ones I'd heard last night screaming in rage. Those two would be trained by Olivier specifically. She handled the tougher turned. I might have been just as unbreakable, but she put my strength to shame. I'd seen her win a fight against vampires decades older than her.

Cameron took my mug and I followed him to the kitchen. He was muttering a mantra under his breath, "Bacon, bacon, bacon, bacon." The kitchen and small cafeteria were bustling with vampires and their companions eating breakfast. Cameron skirted around other people cooking at the stoves and took two plates out of one of the ovens. All the tables in the cafeteria were taken, so after grabbing silverware and drinks, we went outside to eat in the garden.

The outside tables were surrounded by plots of flowers and plenty of lawn in case someone wanted to have a picnic. Othello sat at one of the umbrella-shaded tables with Marie, a younger Born vampire, who was staring at me like I'd insulted her shoes. Being Othello's mate meant power, and Marie wanted that power. She was welcome to it. Hope you enjoy seeing Othello's O-face, Marie. Oh god. Now I was contemplating Othello's O-face.

Cute puppies. Cute puppies.

Cameron and I put everything on a table far away from them and started eating. Cameron had made us Japanese lettuce pancakes with bacon and some kind of sauce on top. My lip curled at the sight of it.

"Stop making a face," he scolded me. "This is good food. Just because it's not blood pudding, or whatever rich ass people ate in the middle ages-" I cut him off by flinging a piece of lettuce pancake at him. He almost looked like he was about to start a food fight, and I was fully prepared to defend my side of the table, when he started laughing and took a big bite of lettuce pancake to spite me. "MMmmmmmm!" he moaned defiantly. Othello and Marie approached us mid-pancake. Marie had a dainty lace parasol in her hand that was the same pink as her stylish suit. Your parasol is pointless, dainty one. Othello wore his typical Victorian getup, looking like a giant tool.

"I left you some daisies in your suite," Othello informed

me, giving me a look like he expected me to suddenly decide to screw him then and there because he'd brought me flowers. Again. For a million days in a row. I made an 'Oh?' face and put pancake in my mouth so I wouldn't say something rude, like 'keep trying, bitch. I will not drop my pants for you.' Unfortunately, as always, he pretended to not notice my lack of exuberance. "After breakfast, we will convene in the dormitory." He turned and walked back towards the castle, rebuffing Marie's attempt to take his arm.

Cameron imitated Othello's deep British accent. *"We will convene in the dormitory."* He rolled his eyes. "Creepy ass dude with his creepy ass accent."

"You know I used to have an accent, right? As did you."

He shrugged his shoulders. "Not a creepy one. What did your accent sound like? You were born in Hungary, right?"

"Transylvania," I corrected since that was what it had been at the time. "As cliché as that sounds. Ugh." I waved my hands around while saying in my Dracula voice, *"Ooo, a vampire born in Transylvania!"* Cameron laughed around a piece of bacon. "I was raised in England, actually. We just managed to stick around in England long enough for the accent to arrive. *Right so, guv-nah.*"

Cameron snorted as Olivier and Renard came around the corner of the castle, arm in arm. Olivier wore a black mermaid dress decorated with leather belts, and she was squinting at the sun like it was there just to torture her. She hated being outside. Renard's broad shoulders dwarfed her small frame and blocked some of the sun.

"We're needed," she said evenly. I couldn't tell if she was dreading it, or was excited at the prospect of working again.

Both. Always both.

I looked down and realized I'd finished the lettuce pancake and it had tasted good, shockingly. Cameron was smirking at me since I was such a picky eater and had eaten something different for once. I flicked more lettuce at him and stood up to follow Olivier to the dormitory.

Taking my spot, Renard sat down with Cameron and they started talking about a TV show they'd both been watching like they were the closest of friends. They had something of a good relationship, considering how long Cameron had been here, and how often they had to entertain themselves while we were busy.

Olivier was quiet on our trek, breaking the silence only to comment on someone's poor fashion choices, and to tell me I had bacon breath. I almost asked what was bothering her, but then I remembered. In a few weeks, new companions would be brought here for the turned and Born to choose from, and that meant the end of all companion contracts. Olivier was probably scared that Renard wouldn't renew his tenure for a fourth time. He wasn't a young man anymore. He was in his mid-40s now. His face was beginning to show thin smile lines, and his buzzed hair was thinning out. Would he really want to spend more years of his life with a woman that he could never have as his own?

Cameron was leaving.

The thought sobered me, and any buzz from the nice

morning was gone. We both entered the dark haunting basement looking like someone had just slapped us. Well. I did, at least. Olivier looked like she was going to punch the next person who was cheerful to her. The atmosphere in front of us was somber, so everyone's face was safe for now. Othello had put on a long black robe, trying to look official as the head of our Order, and he held two large golden keys in his hand. Those keys would unlock every coffin in the room.

Two voices still came from the coffins, screaming faintly, waiting for us to let them out. When they found out we weren't going to, they'd start up again. Logically, we would be doing this ceremony after dark, when the turned couldn't be reduced to a lovely pile of ashes if the sun touched them for too long, but Othello worked on his own schedule. He refused to bend it for the turned.

Olivier and I approached the small group of Born vampires, nodding to the ones we worked with sometimes. Othello silently handed me one of the keys, and he and I walked to the end of the room and began unlocking each coffin, except for the two that were still noisy. It took us a few minutes to reach the other end of the chamber. When we finished, we walked back to the center, where the tall iron candelabras stood.

"Arise," Othello said loudly, his voice echoing. "You are now one of the turned. You have been reborn as a creature of the night." As he spoke, the coffin lids opened one by one and the turned sat up. Their eyes were dark with shadows and each one had a sense of calm they didn't have before now.

They started to step out of the coffins and join us in the center of the room. There were so many, at least fifty, counting the two extras. Every year we turned more and more. The turned were all dirty with old blood, the result of scratching and beating against wood for countless hours.

Olivier led them to the basement shower room, there specifically for the turned to use, while I got to order around some maids. They'd been waiting in the underground garage, a cluster of human housecleaners that did their work and asked no questions. Normally they just cleaned the castle once a week, however, once a year we needed them to change the bedding in the coffins. The turned had done real damage to their interiors, but we'd lined them with old bedding on purpose. Almost every coffin was stripped, given a quick rubdown, and lined with new red silk bedding.

Yes, the turned still slept in the coffins during their training. Only now they wouldn't be locked from the outside. After the maids were done, I led the Born vampires back upstairs to the smaller drawing-room, on the turned side of the house. The room was dimly lit, and red. Red carpet, red curtains, red walls. Red, red, red. Olivier and the turned that had been released were waiting for us, now all cleaned up and dressed in robes. Later today, their measurements would be taken and they would be able to order new clothes for their new bodies.

Othello silenced everyone by clapping his hands. "Now begins your training. You will spend the next five months learning from your instructors, Lisbeth and Olivier." He gestured to us, and I waved with a smile. Olivier ignored everyone. Othello said a few more things, some inspirational bullshit, then he gestured for the Born vampires to leave, and he followed them out.

Their part was done. Now Olivier and I were in charge.

We spent most of the morning answering questions the turned had, and believe me, they were asking the dumbest questions.

Why'd you lock us up?

Are we prisoners?

I don't want to drink blood. It's *gross*.

Olivier's method of dealing with stupidity was chopping their heads off. I was beginning to wish that was acceptable. Our lunch could not have come soon enough, and was brought to us so we could supervise the turned having their new bodies measured.

Olivier bit into a stuffed tomato, her eyes surveying the turned carefully like one might choose to bolt suddenly. I didn't see the point. We were more babysitters than crowd control. Even if they did get past us, they'd burn to a crisp outside.

One of the turned started complaining when it was his turn to be measured, not seeing the point in knowing his size since he didn't care what he wore. Olivier scoffed to herself. "Obviously, we didn't screen well enough," she said quietly.

"Every year these fucks try me. If it's not their endless questions, it's their lack of fashion sense." I rolled my eyes. She was such a fashion diva.

My phone went off and I stuffed a piece of fish in my mouth to lift it out of my pocket. It was a text from Cameron.

Renard wants me to lift weights with him. I THOUGHT WE WERE FRIENDS!!

I giggled and started texting back something witty since Cameron never worked out and still had a perfect body. *Lift weights, flirt with the girls at the gym, and then make him play video games with you :-D*

He responded back with, *Nice try, but there's no girls here. I'm not working out if the gym is lacking ladies.* I laughed and put my phone back in my pocket.

After the measurements were over and the bitching ceased, Olivier and I could begin.

"Your first lesson," I said after everyone had sat down or perched on something, "is your fangs." They all looked disappointed like they'd been expecting something like combat fighting, so I tried to elaborate. "You must know how to control your fangs when you are around a human. Now, I know you have learned control of your thirst, and that's the first step for a turned vampire."

One of the turned interrupted me. "Seriously? We have to sit here and talk about fangs? When do we learn to break stuff?"

Grr.

Olivier answered that one, saving me the chance to tell someone to shut up. "You'll learn that later. It's important right now to learn Vampire etiquette."

"And you only learn to... break things... because it's important to know the boundaries of your strength. Not so you can fight or kill someone," I added quickly.

"That is so boring!" a girl with perfect blonde hair said. She had refused to be measured since she insisted she had always been this skinny. "You mentioned you were a vampire Hunter before," she said to Olivier. "I want to be one."

Olivier's eyebrows knit together. "The turned don't become Hunters."

This outraged several of the turned. "That's so unfair!"

"Why can't we? Is it some super selective club?"

"That's racist!"

Oh my fucking god, I had the worst job in the history of *ever*.

Olivier let out a high-pitched noise that shook the room and made our ears cry with pain. "ALL OF YOU BITCHES SHUT UP!" She straightened and huffed like she was about to send them to detention after spanking their ungrateful asses. "You will all go down to the dormitory. Lessons are over." No one protested.

I walked over to her when the room was empty and wiggled a finger in my ear. "Oww." She smiled as an apology. "I fucking hate it when you do that."

"It gets them to shut the hell up. Worth it," was her response.

My ears disagreed, but I smiled back anyway and pulled her in for a hug. We put our work away and went upstairs. Our companions were in my suite waiting, sitting on one of the divans. Cameron was playing a video game on the big screen TV and Renard was watching him while casually lifting a twenty-pound weight with one arm. They both waved to us, too absorbed to get up. Olivier plopped down on the floor next to Renard and started complaining to him in French about how our day had gone, using every single slur she could think of.

Watching Cameron made me sad again. He'd be gone before I knew it, and I didn't want him to leave me. I quickly grabbed my purse and zipped down to the underground garage for my car. I needed to talk to Balthazar about something, anything. Or I'd find that sweet book reader and have my way with her. Either way, I couldn't be upset about losing my companion. This was a fact of my life.

I stopped at several bookstores, a few antique places, but Balthazar didn't show up. I'd wandered onto the outskirts of town, and was starting to feel weary from my search when I bumped into someone at the end of a street. I started to apologize and noticed it was a child, about ten years old.

The hairs on my neck stood up in warning.

The child stunk of Lycan.

4

A CHILD SPARED

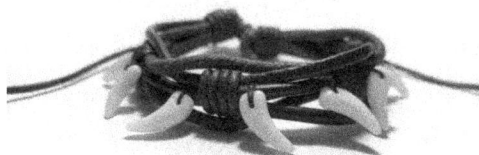

I looked down at the child in front of me. I'd knocked both of us over so I was leaning over him. I sat up and he watched me warily. No doubt, he could smell me as well and knew what I was. His enemy.

"Simon!" someone shouted. I looked up and on the other side of the street crossing were two burly men and a smaller woman that looked just as tough.

Fuck.

I could tell by sight that the taller male was an Alpha. The smell from them made my lips curl in a survival instinct, and I had to fight to keep my fangs from dropping. Why weren't the wolves coming closer? They had an Alpha plus two. I knew I wouldn't stand much of a chance against them. They could easily run over here, grab me and the child, and rip me to pieces in a dark alley. I looked down at the child and back at the Lycans, and then it hit me.

The borders. The edge of my Order's land was this street crossing. The border we owned spread the same distance in every direction and it was marked by the scent of vampire blood. The Lycans couldn't cross to save their pup or their lives would be forfeit to me. It was the law.

I looked back down at the boy. His scent was human, I realized. The Lycan scent I'd smelled was residual, from other people. His parents. The boy had black hair and tanned skin, a typical werewolf look. His features were in-between boy and preteen. He still had the chubby cherub cheeks and full lips of a child, but his eyes were deep and aged. He knew running from me wouldn't do any good. He was waiting for me to take him away and do my duty.

And fuck me, I couldn't do it.

"Simon," I said to him over the very few humans around us, hoping that that was his name. "I am over four hundred years old. And in all that time, I have never killed a child. I'm not saying I've never killed before because I have." I stole a glance at the Lycans and they were listening with straining ears to hear me. "I have drained the blood of innocents and thought nothing of it. But my hands have never harmed a child." I stood up and held my hand out to him. He took it and let me lead him to the edge of the border, in the middle of the street. There were no cars around, so the Lycans met us in the center.

The Alpha regarded me with cautious eyes. "Why are you

letting the boy go? He crossed. He is surrendered to you now. His blood is yours to spill." The boy's mother was holding back a sob, pretending she was growling at me. Her mate put his arm on her shoulder to steady her.

I met the Alpha's gaze, suddenly feeling brave while sizing up a Lycan so big he made me look like a toothpick. "You heard what I said. I will not spill a child's blood. Not even a Lycan." I tried not to say Lycan like it was a dirty word. Simon's hand was still in mine, I released it and gave him a push to his parents. They grabbed him fiercely, giving me a look like they'd fight me if I changed my mind.

"Your kind will find out," the Alpha warned me.

"I don't smell anyone nearby," I told him, making sure to breathe deeply and push my senses out around us. "And if you left, it would be even better for both of us. So leave. Now." I gestured with my hand in the opposite direction of where we were standing.

Instead of just leaving like Simon and his parents were doing, the Lycan Alpha handed me a bracelet he'd just removed from his wrist. It was easily almost three times the width of my own delicate wrists. "We owe you a debt, blood-sucker. Keep this, and it will protect you from any Lycan that tries to harm you."

I turned the bracelet over in my hands. It was very intricate with braided threads and beads, and... "Are those *fucking vampire teeth*??" I tried not to be too horrified since he was trying to thank me, but damn it was difficult.

He smiled ruefully. "They are a symbol of strength and status."

"That's kind of bullshit," I whispered to myself and almost gave it back, but he chuckled at me and was gone. The bracelet stunk of Lycan and I found a public restroom to wash it clean until it smelled like vanilla soap before stuffing it in my pocket.

I went home and pretended nothing had happened. As far as I could tell, I was in the clear. No one knew I'd broken our second highest law. The first was about not killing another vampire. I hid the bracelet in my room. I seriously wasn't about to wear something with vampire teeth on it as a decoration. Symbol of strength, my ass.

Olivier unlocked the two remaining turned the next morning. They were large men with ripples of muscles, and they were strong. Stronger than I was. It was a shame they were one of the turned. They would've been invaluable if they were Born. With the addition to the ranks, we took the opportunity to introduce the strength lesson early.

After dark, we led the turned out to a small clearing beyond the castle grounds. It was lit with gas lamps that looked like the color of firefly light. One lamp flickered, so Olivier walked up and kicked it. It flickered again and came back on stronger than before like it was afraid Olivier would kick it again. She hopped onto a fallen log and I walked up to stand beside her as she got the group's attention.

"Today we're learning about the limitations of our strength. It's important to know the exact limits of strength in order to keep it under control. You can't be in control if you're afraid of breaking someone or something all the time. So. Go pick a tree, and have fun." She gestured to the forest behind us. "Don't worry. We sell any trees you knock down and plant new ones later. You two," she added, pointing her finger at the two bigger turned. "With me." They followed her, and one of them glanced over at me and waved with his pointer finger.

The other turned quickly began their strength lesson, and it was my job to supervise and motivate them. They started hitting the trees, softly at first, but then they really started giving it their all.

"Don't be afraid to punch it! It won't hit you back. No," I told one of them. "Put your thumb on the outside of your fingers. You'll cut into your palm if you– Damn it! No punching other students! *Oh my god!*" Someone started laughing behind me, and I turned to see Balthazar standing next to one of the gas lamps. He swung his cane at me as a hello. Everyone was busy with their exercises, so I left the turned and crossed the clearing to join him.

"Hey," I said as I got closer. "What are you doing here?" I squinted at him, trying to figure out his motives. "Don't tell me. The restriction is lifted and you want to tell me all about the human girl you just fucked behind Arby's?"

He sighed wearily, no traces of amusement on his face. "Am I not allowed to visit you whenever I choose?"

I blinked. He was never not cheerful. And he also never came to the castle. "Umm, of course you are."

"I'm just checking up on you," he said quietly, his face softening and looking more normal. "You're busy though, so I'll leave." I started to protest, but he was gone and there was no way to call him back. Damn it. It was about time he got a mobile so this would stop happening.

"What was that about?" Olivier asked, suddenly right in my ear. I screamed and jumped three feet in the air, then came crashing down, only to land on one of my heels. I heard a snap that wasn't my leg.

"Fuck!" I shouted, peering down at my shoe. Olivier bent to examine it and said with a sigh of relief, "not designer," as if that meant breaking it wasn't a big deal. Though, if they had been designer, I'd have been more upset. I hobbled to the log she'd stood on earlier and sat down to inspect my broken shoe.

Speaking of breaking.

"You might want to..." I pointed to her big charges that were launching tree trunks at other trees and starting to launch them at each other.

"Son of a bitch! QUIT THAT RIGHT NOW, YOU FUCKING HOOLIGANS!"

I laughed under my hand, pretending to cough. Frustrated Olivier was always entertaining, but she didn't appreciate me giggling about it. The turned continued for several hours, making the small clearing into a bigger one with the effort. We still had a while until dawn, but by then we were all as exhausted as we can get. The turned walked back to the castle with us at their heels. I hobbled beside Olivier with my broken shoe. She was about to make a snarky comment about my boots but stopped when we opened the rear gate and entered the back garden.

Othello stood with a few older vampires, discussing something intense. Among them stood a tall, muscled Born I'd never seen before. We walked closer, catching their attention. Everyone's gaze was business as usual, except for the new Born. He stared at us with cold icy blue eyes like he was looking for the person who stole his cookies, and we had cookie crumbs on us. Olivier went rigid beside me and gave him an equally pensive look. She was momentarily the Hunter Olivier, the side of her I'd never been around, and if her face was anything to go by, I wasn't sure I wanted to.

"Ladies, there you are." Othello motioned us closer. The Born's eyes followed us as if he expected us to bolt away. "This is Arthur," Othello said, waving a hand towards the hawk-like vampire beside him. Arthur's clothing was decorated with a horde of weapons strapped to his limbs and waist. His face and arms had a few tattoos and several nasty looking scars, but it only made him look more virile, and annoyingly, slightly attractive.

Yes. He was *super* hot. I'd have to get his number.

Arthur finally spoke, his voice deep and rough. "Olivier and I are acquainted." His inflection on acquainted spoke of

45

more than simple friendship, but his expression remained neutral. Staring into his cold eyes, I found myself wondering if he was capable of any emotion other than disinterested. What would happen if I kissed him?

"If you'll excuse us, Lisbeth and I are exhausted. Good night." Olivier grabbed my arm and herded me through the back door. I tried to speak several times, but she continued to hush me until we'd reached my suite. Cameron was asleep in his room so the parlor was empty. Olivier sank down into a chair and sighed heavily. I didn't say anything, just sat on the couch next to her chair, and waited for her to explain. She peeked over at me and then looked at the ceiling. "Arthur is a Hunter. A special kind of Hunter, I should say. When he arrives, he's looking for a criminal that's part of an Order. And he never *EVER* shows up at an Order unless someone has broken the law."

Oh. *SHIT*.

Arthur was here for me. The tall sexy beast I'd contemplated kissing was here for *me*. And not in the good way.

I tried not to tense at her words, and failed. She sat up straight to appraise me blankly. "Something you'd like to share with the class? You know I'm trained to notice even the slightest hint of body language, right?"

Oh, I knew. I'd once attempted to pull off a lie in front of her, and it didn't go very well. When I met her gaze, I couldn't help but display a small measure of guilt. She stared at me for a long time, waiting for me to explain, but I kept my mouth shut. Admitting what I'd done would mean

Olivier might be punished as well. Besides, I was being irrational. Just because lawbreaking was rare didn't mean it never happened. Arthur might be here for someone else. Maybe.

"So," she said slowly, dragging the word out. "Keeping secrets? Secrets are shit. No one is allowed to have secrets."

I almost laughed. "Not even Renard?"

"Never." She dropped it, seeing that I wouldn't be confessing anytime soon. I couldn't tell whether she suspected me or thought I knew who the culprit was.

***

The next day I found Arthur walking around on the west side of the building where the full-sized chess set was. He lifted up the king piece easily and looked inside its hollow center.

"I don't think there's a criminal in there," I informed him, pointing to the empty space. He set it down and reached to pick up the rook to search it too. "I'm Lisbeth, by the way."

"Hmm," he said in response, and picked up another piece to study. "I'm busy, Lisbeth. Go bother someone else." Arthur's voice was deep and rough like he'd shouted too much or hardly used his vocal chords, but he also lacked the tonal quality that made voices nice to listen to. He was truly cold inside and out.

"Rude," I muttered and climbed onto the rook to sit on top of it, watching the Hunter check the chess field like a moron. He had sandy blonde hair cropped close to his head and his jaw looked like it was chiseled from stone. Je-sus. I was still attracted to him. Wrong place, wrong Hunter. "So you dated Olivier, huh?"

"We didn't *date*," he said blankly, finally looking my way.

"Oh, so you mean you just..." I mimed sex with my fingers. He watched me and raised an eyebrow, then picked up a pawn to look at.

"That was a long time ago." He moved to the white side of the board, where I was sitting.

"Are you with anyone now?" God, I was really going there. Be still my loins. He wasn't worth it.

"I'm on the job," he informed me shortly and picked up the rook with me still on it. "Besides, you're not my type. I prefer women who aren't airheads." Oh no he didn't.

He set me down with a thunk and I jumped off, grabbing his dog tag necklace to bring that chiseled jaw towards my face. "Airhead I am not, sir." His blue eyes looked my face up and down, and I instantly regretted being this close to him. My body was heating up and I found myself wanting to test that kiss theory. Would he melt in my arms, or push me away? I let go of his tags and stepped back to the rook. "They tell me you only come here when one of us has broken a law." I tried to look casual. The chess piece search forgotten, Arthur leaned against a pawn.

"That's true. I prefer to not be amongst all the..." He wiggled his hand, but I wasn't going to let him be vague.

I crossed my hands over my chest. "Amongst all the what?"

"Castle. Money. Cars. Jewelry. Your kind. Stuffy rich vampires."

"I am not *stuffy*," I huffed. Now I wasn't sure if I wanted to kick him or plant my body against his until he surrendered to me.

He snorted, hiding the smile, and pointed a finger at me. "Oh yeah? How much did your shoes cost?"

"*Fuck you!*" I shouted and stormed off across the lawn.

5

ARTHUR'S PREY

*D*ays passed, and I tried to wipe Arthur from my mind. Lying in bed, my mind kept flashing images of the Lycan Alpha and the brown-eyed pup I'd saved. I'd hidden the bracelet behind the drawer in my nightstand, and for some reason, I felt like taking it out. Twirling it around my fingers, I admired the bracelet, as it truly was a fine piece of work, despite the insulting teeth woven into it. I tried to pretend they belonged to a cat. A very large cat.

I'd just drifted off to sleep with the bracelet still in my hand when there was a pounding at the door. My blood turned cold. Was Arthur here to arrest me? I quickly used the bracelet to tie my hair back and then covered it with a wide ribbon so no one could see it before putting on a robe. Cameron was answering the door when I walked into the parlor, and in burst Arthur, followed by his security team.

Othello entered behind them, protesting loudly. "I told you that Lisbeth cannot possibly be the-" He was cut off by Arthur's hand rising as a signal to shut up.

"Everyone is suspect. No exceptions," Arthur informed him.

Without even asking me, the Born security team swept over my rooms. They took care to not break anything, thankfully, but they didn't care about replacing pillowcases after they'd been removed or putting my belongings back in an orderly fashion.

I played it cool and kept my face neutral like I was simply annoyed at being bothered. "Anything in particular you're looking for?" I asked him casually.

Arthur had stayed in the parlor with us, probably monitoring our reactions. "Evidence," he replied, like it was obvious. He glanced at me and his eyes went south, his mouth twitching a few times. My robe was open, so I closed it quickly. Under these circumstances, I didn't want him staring at me. Stuffy, indeed.

"He's searched everyone else's rooms as well," Othello mentioned from the doorway, no doubt trying to make me feel better. It didn't work. I knew exactly what Arthur was doing. He was an experienced Hunter who didn't need to bother looking for evidence. Searching our rooms was just a pretense to appease whoever had sent him. Once nothing incriminating was found, the criminal would relax and slip up somehow, and then Arthur would have him. Or her.

The security group finished, having only found a naked

mermaid statue in Cameron's bathroom that held a stash of money. Othello led the team out and onto the next suite, but Arthur didn't move from his spot on my carpet.

"You didn't answer the door."

"I was asleep." He was squinting at me, and I really wanted to slap him for it. "Being stuffy is exhausting, you know."

He wasn't amused. "It wasn't the first room we searched. You didn't hear us?" he observed, scratching at his stubble.

Cameron was the one who spoke up and saved me. "Dude, these walls are ridiculously soundproof. Do you know how many times the couple next door bangs? We don't, because we don't hear it."

It occurred to me that Arthur knew all of this. He was simply testing my reactions. He was nothing if not thorough. And that meant he was close to being onto me. Thankfully, he left soon afterward, and we all went back to bed as if nothing had happened.

Stupid Arthur with his stupid searches trying to get under my skin. I was confident that I would be able to get him off my scent and on his merry way. I even entertained that he wasn't here for me, though I didn't discount it. I mean, who had even seen me at the border? I hadn't smelled anyone nearby at the time.

However, if anyone had seen me, even a human, our kind could find out. Since it involved drinking excess blood and using our powers on humans, it would be technically against the law, which was ironic. Breaking the law to find out who broke the law. It all depended on how far Hunters could go to keep us in line. I supposed it was a grey area for them. They got exceptions for all kinds of things. Mind controlling humans might be in that category. I had a slight hope that such methods were not allowed, even for them.

The next morning, I spent ten minutes finding the best way to hide the bracelet on my person without someone noticing, just in case Arthur searched my rooms again. Why was I even keeping it? My intuition overruled my logic since some part of me wanted to hang on to it. I finally went with fastening it to a garter belt.

I forced myself to relax when I went downstairs after feeding from Cameron. Even he was noticing my off behavior, so when I joined Olivier in the dining hall, I tried to pretend like nothing was wrong.

Arthur was sitting next to her.

Be cool, be cool.

He didn't react when I approached. I sat next to Renard, who was clearly annoyed that his lady was sitting next to another man. I avoided all body language that indicated hiding something and lying. My body felt stiff from sitting a certain way all the time. The way Arthur was staring at me was unnerving, like he was hunting and I was his prey. I can't deny the feeling that invoked deep inside me, making my face flush under his gaze, but this wasn't the time to react to him because I might actually be his prey, and not in the good way.

"Hey hey," I greeted as I unrolled my napkin and put it in my lap. No one spoke. Olivier picked at her food and stared at a spot behind me. She too looked unusually stiff. "So," I said slowly. "Arthur. Where are you going after you catch the lawbreaker?"

He turned his frigid blue eyes to me like I'd just spit on him, and I had to physically hold my breath to keep from displaying any damning signals.

"What?" he asked blankly.

I saw Olivier's eyes dart to me, and then back at whatever she was fixated on. "I mean, you won't stay here afterward, right?"

"No." He liked single word responses.

"Maybe we should all go to town before you leave," I continued. "Do you like movies?"

"Not really," he responded. I went back to eating my food in silence since my table mates were doing the same. After a long period of quiet, Arthur said, "You're awfully chatty, Lisbeth."

I shrugged. "Am I not allowed to talk to people?" Goddd. He was going to smell this lie on me like perfume. I sucked at everything.

Instead of answering, he got up and took his dishes to the

sink. Olivier waited until he had left the room before she relaxed. She gave me a pursed look.

"Stop sitting like that. You look uncomfortable." I slacked my spine a bit. "And stop talking to him. It won't go well." She picked at her salad. "He told me you tried flirting with him."

"*What?* I did not. That is outlandish, how dare you!"

"You use big words when you're flustered."

"You suck, I'm leaving." I stood up and left the cafeteria as fast as I could.

After that, it took effort, but I managed to maintain a normal attitude and continued with the turned training for the next few days. Arthur was never far away. I dreaded when he would show up, seemingly out of nowhere, and then watch me for hours. My only consolation was when I saw him doing the same thing to a few other Born vampires. Sickeningly, the small group of female vampires he was cornering all had the same hair color. My hair color. I looked down at my thick black curls and knew. It was as I feared.

Arthur was here for me.

The thought was relaxing and terrifying all at the same time. On the one hand, I knew all along that he was here for me. It also dashed my hopes that I was wrong.

Olivier had never told me what happened to lawbreaking

vampires when the Hunters caught them. She only said it wasn't pleasant. I assumed it was decapitation or something similar. No trial before the heads of the Orders. Who cared if they were falsely accused or were in the wrong place at the wrong time? I could tell Arthur killed and asked questions never.

I stood in the shadow of the castle, thinking of what my next move would be when Olivier drove up in her convertible.

"Get in, loser. We're going shopping."

I jumped in and we sped away. Olivier drove to the nearby town and kept going past the city limits.

"Arthur was sent here to find you," she said finally. Of course she knew. I hadn't even tried to fool her, as if I could. "I've known for days."

"He recruited you to help him." Sigh. Such an underhanded move from such a sexy guy.

"Gods help me, I had no choice, Lisbeth. The heads of the Order commanded it. He told me someone had spared a Lycan that crossed the borders, and he was sent to find out who it was. We've been drinking extra blood and interrogating dozens of humans in the town. We eventually found what we needed. The humans that were there that day remembered you. Black curls. Purple eyes." I shut my eyes and curled my fingers around the bracelet, still strapped to my leg. "Why, Lisbeth?" she demanded, slamming her hand on the steering wheel in frustration. "*Fuck.* Why would you break the law?"

I opened my eyes and stared at the road in front of us. "He was a child, Olivier. If there's only one rule I can live by in my long life, it's protecting the life of a child."

"Shit." She smashed both palms down on the steering wheel, looking away in frustration. "You've risked every-thing. *Everything.*"

Reality slipped into me, like a cold icicle down my throat. Everything with Arthur had distracted me from the real danger, and now I couldn't avoid it any longer. "I know."

"I can't protect you," she said. I could hear tears in her voice.

"I know," I repeated. I wanted to apologize, but that would mean I regretted it. And I didn't.

She casually ran a hand across her face. "Backseat," she said. I unbuckled myself and leaned over the backseat. There was a huge duffel bag in the floorboard. The duffel bag she'd brought with her when she came to our Order, an ex-Hunter with no sense of our way of life. I sat back down with it in my lap.

"We going camping?" I asked, half confused. She abruptly pulled the car over into a little roadside park and stopped.

"You have a choice. Right now. You run. You run like there's a forest fire licking your ankle. And you never look back. You never stop running."

That sounded exhausting. "Or?"

"I take you back to the Order, and you face Arthur's justice."

We sat there as I weighed both options. I realized that

while I didn't regret what I'd done, I didn't want to die. I really didn't. When I'd saved the child, I thought no one would ever know, and now I would be paying for it with my life.

"I'll run," I told her.

6

OLIVIER'S LIST OF SURVIVAL

*O*livier left me at the roadside park with very few parting words. Don't tell her my plans, and follow the list in the duffel bag. She had to get back to the castle and pretend she hadn't just helped me escape. Fooling Arthur seemed to be part of her skillsets. I wasn't worried.

Alone, and miles away from the nearest town, I took the list out and started walking down the highway.

Olivier's list of survival

1. Get a car.

Seemed simple enough.

2. Pick something in-between what you'd pick for yourself and what you'd never drive.

So something between 'car' and 'Hummer.' Got it.

3. There are sneakers in the bag.

Thank god. I took my heels off and replaced them with

the sneakers. Much better. Running for my life wouldn't be much fun in heels.

4. *Stop reading the list and follow number 1.*

I rolled my eyes and stuck the list into my pocket.

It was survival time. I had to rearrange my way of thinking. Whatever the Hunters and Arthur thought I was going to do, I would have to do the opposite. Or was that completely wrong and stupid? Would they expect that of me? Don't overthink it.

They probably expected me to steal a car and then leave a trail of stolen cars for them to follow. A trail was not a good idea. After an hour of walking on back roads, I reached a town. I rummaged through the duffle bag and found a plastic baggie with a large amount of cash in it, enough to buy a car. Or maybe two cars.

After asking around, I found a used car place that looked semi-shady, one that wouldn't ask questions or require paperwork, and would keep their mouths shut with the proper encouragement. I bought something tiny, expensive, and probably extremely gas efficient. Definitely not me at all. The dealer charged me double and I didn't break his arm for it, even though I was sorely tempted to. The money baggie was still semi-full when I left in my tiny car.

The day was far from over and I was already exhausted. My feet had blisters from walking so far. I could feel Cameron's blood working on them, leaving me hungry and cranky. I'd only need a sip or two and it would be fixed. The duffle bag didn't have clothing in it, meaning I had to purchase all of that myself.

I drove another hour and then raided a hippy clothing store where the clerk looked so out of it, I bet she didn't even remember what I looked like. I changed in my car and turned the Alpha's bracelet over and over in my hands. A simple act had started all this, but no matter what, I refused to feel regret. The bracelet was made for a large arm and I wrapped it around my wrist a few times until it wouldn't fall off. Once I was a few hours away from the Order, I pulled over and looked at everything in the duffle bag. Besides the money baggie, there was a large container of unmarked lotion, which was addressed in the list.

5. *Use this so you'll look more human.*

The lotion, as I found out, would tint my white skin so I would appear human. I applied it liberally all over my body. Goodbye, pale skin. Hello, tan.

6. *Dye your hair.*

I recoiled. I didn't want to dye my hair. Call it pride, but I loved my black curls. They were part of me. Who would I be without them?

7. *No buts.*

Damn you, Olivier! The list had a few tips on other things I'd need to survive, and ended with one line.

18. *I believe in you.*

With a smidge more confidence than I had before, I drove for another hour before going to a beauty parlor. I was already in another state by now, and my route wasn't a straight line, so I felt safe that I'd lost Arthur for now. The beautician gave me a trim before chemically straightening my hair and dying it dark brown.

Dressed in earthy, beachy tree hugger clothing with no makeup, and my beautiful curls straightened and dyed brown, and my skin a golden orange, the face I saw in the mirror every day was gone. I felt ugly and plain. My reflection in the beauty parlor mirror was a stranger. Would I lose myself in all of this? Would running away erase all I'd become in 400 years? I couldn't think about that right now.

Numbly, I left the beauty parlor and bought a pair of sunglasses, a snack, and a map from a sidewalk vendor. My new car was waiting at the end of the block. It needed a name. All good vessels did. This car was going to carry me to safety, away from Arthur and his chiseled jaw.

I dub thee Excalibur.

While munching on some churros, I used the map to plot a route to the safest place I could think of. Texas. It was mostly pack territory, and that worked to my advantage. I didn't know exactly where the packs lived, but I would know when I got there. They mark their territory, and I'm not using an idiom. They literally piss on it. Yuck.

And even though I was nervous, scared, and self-doubting, I still felt oddly excited. I'd been living in luxury for more than a century, so using my wit to survive wasn't needed. Even before then, I'd always relied on other vampires to make the decisions for me, except for my sabbatical when I was still a fledgling. That didn't really count though, because right after leaving my home in England, I'd met Olivier and then followed her around for decades. It's a good thing she stopped thinking I was annoying.

Maybe I'd just been waiting for something like this. Something to finally rip me from my mundane life and force me to start living in the moment. To show myself, not just Arthur, that I wasn't stuffy.

Being on the run was invigorating. I'd forgotten how good it felt. The danger of it all seeped into my veins and I felt like I was drowning in adrenaline. As much as I was loving it, I still missed my simple life at the Order. I missed spending time with Cameron. It was comforting to know he was safe, though. I tried to put him out of my mind. I tried to picture him living a normal human life. Getting a job. A house. A wife. He'd finally belong. That was all I wanted for him.

My new car was adorable. Sleeping in it was not. A quick purchase of a down sleeping bag made the small trunk more comfortable, though my long legs didn't thank me for it. I slept at highway truck stops and applied the tanning lotion every morning.

That became my schedule. Wake up, drive. Eat food, drive. Eat again, park somewhere hidden, sleep. Repeat.

The one thing Olivier hadn't provided for me was blood. I was starving for blood, but I couldn't feed. Finding a human wouldn't work because a human's first vampire bite took days to heal. If I stole disgusting bagged blood from a hospital, the Hunters would find out. Any blip of stolen blood on a hospital record and they'd be on that hospital like a swarm of bees. It was on the list as things to avoid doing, but I needed blood. If I didn't feed soon, I'd go into a frenzy, and that was a shit storm I'd never escape from. I stopped at a large city that I could blend into and scoured it until I found a blood drive. It was at a large Catholic church in the parking lot. Groups of old people and families stood outside the little trailer, all sipping juice and eating cookies as they talked amongst themselves.

The lady at the sign-in table was wearing pastel cashmere and a big smile that silently promised it would try to convert me later. Not gonna happen, sister. I signed a fake name and went into the trailer when it was my turn. A nurse stood inside and showed me where to sit. There was an old man next to me who had fallen asleep in his chair. His blood bag was almost full. I tried not to stare at it.

The nurse tried chatting to me in a friendly way as she gathered some paperwork for me to fill out. I saw an open ice chest of filled blood bags on a tray in front of me and saw my chance.

I stood up and pretended I was off balance. "Actually, I don't feel so good. I'm really squeamish, and I was trying to face my fears, but I just-" I dry heaved and put my hand on the side of the ice chest, purposefully knocking it over. "I'm so sorry!" I pretended to try to pick them up, and 'accidentally' stepped on a few until they popped. The smell of dead blood shot up my nose. I felt equally sick and hungry.

I almost felt sorry for the human nurse, having to deal with me standing in a pile of half busted blood bags and heaving like I was about to throw up. I repeatedly told her I was sorry and made sure to look as pathetic as possible. I helped her gather the bags back into the ice chest, and told her I'd throw them away.

As if.

I went out the back door of the trailer, where the happy humans couldn't see me with blood all over my hands and shoes, and ran in the other direction. I hid behind the dumpster and took stock of what I had to work with.

Out of four bags, three were busted and only had a small amount of blood left in them. The fourth bag was fine. All that effort for one bag of blood. It figured. I left them there, dropped the ice chest back off behind the trailer, and went back for my bounty. I stuck to the shadows on my way back to Excalibur, sucking on the busted bags until they were dry. I found a puddle to wiggle my shoes in to clean them. I saw myself in the reflection, blood all over my arms. As much as it disgusted me, I licked myself clean. Every drop was ecstasy.

Mission accomplished. Score for Lisbeth.

FRENZIED

*B*agged blood is revolting.

It's like having a mug of tea that smells like tea and looks like tea, but when you sip it, it tastes like dog piss. My brain constantly reminded me that this was not what blood is supposed to taste like. Not to mention it made me feel sick. Never throw up sick, but a headache and general lethargy were the main side effects. I honestly had no idea how the turned could live on this stuff, but they could. Lucky fucks.

After a week of zigzagging, backtracking, carefully timed slow poking, occasional sitting around for hours, and swearing so loudly I was sure the humans were going to call the cops, I was in Kansas. The bagged blood was making my temples throb. I'd rationed myself to one sip a day, but I was paying the price. Weakness was spreading throughout my body, a paralyzing weakness that sometimes hit me so hard I couldn't move my arms to get the blood from the cooler in the morning. I was also losing weight, and my eyes were constantly bloodshot like I was drunk.

After passing the Kansas state sign, I was sitting in Excalibur at a roadside park, carefully forcing myself to sip some blood from the pack after fumbling with it for a few minutes because my fingers refused to work. God, it tasted foul. My mouth scrunched up and I gagged, like a human taking medicine. Nasty gross 'please leave my stomach' medicine.

'Heat of the Moment' came from the backseat. Why was my car playing music? It started playing again, and I realized it was coming from the duffle bag. Hidden in one of the numerous side pockets was an old-fashioned burner phone and one of those wireless chargers that ran on batteries. Amazingly, the phone still had a percentage on the battery and wasn't dead even though it had been sitting in my car for a week.

As the song started a third time, I answered the phone.

"Hello?" I had no idea who would be on the other end. Arthur? He would. Maybe it was a booty call? Arthur booty calling me. Nah.

"*Bonjour*, Lisbeth." Renard.

I sighed with relief. I wasn't in the mood for sexy talk. "Renard! Why are you calling me? I'm on the run!"

"I know. It was Olivier who was going to call you, but..." He trailed off and his silence was deafening. I immediately thought she'd been killed or punished for helping me, but then he wouldn't be there to call me. "All Hunters have been recruited to find you. Including former Hunters," he added.

Oh. Olivier hunting me? I mean, she'd been helping Arthur at the castle, but hunting me in the open was completely different. That was the least amount of comforting information I could've ever gotten. My hands shook and I almost dropped the phone. "If she leads them off my trail for too long, they'll know she's helping me."

"*Oui.*" He sighed and struggled for words. "I do not wish to compromise your safety by asking this, but please... protect my lady." My heart broke for him. To protect her, I would have to use a different tactic, and that meant I could become vulnerable. Fuck it, I was smart. I could figure it out.

"I'll do my best," I promised him.

"How are you doing without blood?"

I swallowed and took some time to answer. "Fine," I lied. Lying was stupid, and I knew it. I could hear him silently calling me out on trying to bullshit him. Renard had been with us for a long time. While he'd never seen for himself the side effects of our hunger, he knew well enough from stories we'd told him. Before I could speak, he had to hang up and get back to the castle.

So. I had to come up with an entirely new plan, one that would protect both Olivier and myself. I took a break from eating gas station food and went to a country café. They had some maps of Kansas and the nearby states, so I bought one of each. While I ate a greasy hamburger with fries and a red soda (it wasn't blood, but the color was comforting), I plotted out a new route and made new plans. The constant planning and sneaking around was wearing me out, even without the bagged blood sapping all my energy. Olivier probably knew that and would inform Arthur, so continuing with my path was the best option.

The next night, I was at another rest stop finishing up a few sips of vile blood when I smelled vampires.

Shit on a stick.

They'd found me. I knew it. My stupid plans were for shit and now I'd be captured. I pushed my senses out and caught the scent of leather and steel. Definitely Hunters. They weren't close enough to be able to smell me as well unless they were paying attention. I drove away in Excalibur and found an unpaved driveway that lead to an empty house with a rundown barn. I parked Excalibur inside the barn and doused the car in a spray that would mask my scent (it was in the duffle bag), then I started running. I ran as fast as I could and my senses widened automatically without me having to use energy. Running was taxing, and my feet stumbled every other step. I couldn't keep it up much longer. My senses were starting to close back in from my lack of blood. I started tripping and struggled to focus. Blackness came up on the edges of my sight. Then I smelled it.

Blood.

Sweet, fresh blood flowing in a human's vulnerable papery veins. I could've wept with joy at my discovery. Why did it smell so weird? Humans didn't smell like that. My need overrode my sense of smell, and a frenzy swept over me. In the days before companions, this kind of frenzy was commonplace, and we did our best to avoid it. There was no stopping me. I would be drinking from this food source whether it fucking liked it or not.

Closer and closer to my prey, I found myself creeping up on a small alcove carved into a rock formation. The oddly smelling human had made a camp inside the alcove, complete with a fire and a rabbit cooking over it. I had lost most of my control and was behaving with a primal edge. My canines dropped and I growled low in my throat. My prey was instantly alert, somehow hearing me.

I charged and threw myself onto my prey, snarling with elation. The human tried to pull me off, but I'd sunk my claws into it. Him. The human was male. He smelled so fucking good, I couldn't control myself. He backed up and slammed both of us into the wall of the cave. Pain crashed into me and my instincts gave me one final push.

I sank my fangs into his neck and moaned as his essence filled my mouth. Gods above, yes. Finally, blood. Tasting it after so long was almost erotic. He groaned and stopped trying to buck me off, going still under my fangs. His blood didn't taste normal, but it wasn't a bad taste. It was like eating venison. If I'd been saner during that precise moment, I'd have been horrified about comparing humans to food. Wild Me didn't care. I drank four times the amount of blood I normally needed. It was only then I regained enough control to pull away and drop the human on the ground.

He wasn't dead, I hadn't drunk that much. He also wasn't

moving, so that wasn't a good sign. He had thick black hair almost to his neck and his skin was one shade darker than a really good tan. He definitely had Native blood. My senses returned and my head stopped hurting. It was then I noticed one crucial detail about my prey I'd been too frenzied to notice before.

He was a Lycan.

8

AN UNUSUAL PAIRING

*O*f all the fucking gin caves in all the world, I had to pick one with a *fucking Lycan*. In my defense, this particular Lycan smelled different than others I'd encountered. I mean, yeah, he had the dog smell. No denying that. But it wasn't all dog. There was human mixed with it. And the more I studied him, the more human he looked. A very attractive human, I noted. Maybe he'd picked up the smell from someone else. Why did I think he was a Lycan? Maybe the starvation had messed with my head. I should've been instantly alerted to his species, even during a frenzy. I'd only been staring at him for a few minutes when he stirred and instantly jumped away from me.

"Who the fucking hell are you?" he demanded. His hand went up to his neck and he found the puncture wounds. I hadn't left any blood on him. Call me greedy. "You... *fucking bit me!*" He lunged at me in anger and slammed me into the wall. "God damn blood sucking harlot, I should kill you right now!" His arm was pressed against my neck, cutting off my air. I slapped at him to get him to lay off, but he refused.

"Watch with the name calling, fuzzy butt," I got out between breaths.

"Shut up, bloodsucker! You have five seconds to tell me why I shouldn't slit your throat right here." I lifted my hand again to try and pull his arm off my throat. The bracelet jingled and he went very still when he saw it. "Where'd you get that?"

My throat was starting to hurt from the abuse. "You take your arm off my neck and I'll tell you." He lessened the pressure slightly. "Thank you. I'm Lisbeth by the way. What's your name?" His dark brown eyes were eyeing me with caution, and I reminded myself that he was a *gross* Lycan. I was a sucker for brown eyes.

"Knight," he offered stoically. "Tell me the truth, bloodsucker. Did you kill the Lycan that owned the bracelet?" I shook my head and he pushed off the wall, taking a few steps back so he wouldn't have to be so close to me. I coughed and felt my throat for a bit, wincing at the pain. "I think I bruised you," he observed, peering over at me.

"Yeah, thank you for that." *God.* He didn't have to hurt me. I mean, I did drink without asking. I guess I would've done the same.

73

"Let me see," he said quietly and held up his hands to gently probe at my neck. "They're going away. I'm uhh... sorry." He stepped back and I observed him cautiously, slightly scared he'd hurt me again.

"To be fair we are enemies," I noted, finding a smile despite the pain. He smiled back and I felt the air leave my chest at the sight of it. Before I could contemplate why I was staring at him like he was a bar of chocolate, Knight quickly grabbed me and clamped a hand over my face. Fuck, I knew I shouldn't have trusted him.

Knight's skin was very warm, almost too hot, and dirty. Gross. I made a small noise to complain at the state of his hand, but he shushed me and pulled me further back into the cave, my backside against his front.

Was that a phone in his pocket? Please be a phone.

"Answer with a nod," he whispered into my ear. "Are they here for you?" By 'they,' he meant the Hunters that I'd been trying to avoid, who had somehow followed my trail here. Damn it! I'd been so careful! Did I have to spray myself with human sweat? I nodded to him. Knight quickly pushed me onto the floor, covered me with his sleeping bag, and sat on top of me with his probably hairy Lycan ass.

My voice was muffled by the sleeping bag, but I managed to get out, "I'm going to fucking murder you!"

"Not with my stolen blood in your veins you're not!" We both grew silent when the Hunters approached within hearing range. I couldn't see them from under the sleeping bag so I waited patiently, trusting this wolf with my life. If he betrayed me, I'd have to slice that handsome face open. A shame, really.

"I didn't know there were *bitches* in this neck of the woods," one of the Hunters remarked as he drew closer.

"You sure it's a dog, Mal?" a woman said, her voice jeering and taunting. "He doesn't smell like a dog." Speaking of smell, why hadn't they caught my scent? Hiding under a sleeping bag wasn't going to stop them from smelling me. Unless Knight's scent was blocking mine. His sleeping bag was soaked with his odor.

"He smells delicious," a third Hunter drawled out. She sounded like she wanted more from Knight than his blood. Good. I wasn't the only vampire smelling that scent.

Blood! They'd see the bite mark on his neck! They'd know I was here! I must've stiffened because Knight moved his hand to cover my shoulder. I couldn't tell if he was trying to be reassuring, or didn't want to blow our cover.

"What do you want, bloodsuckers?" Knight's voice was smooth and warm, the opposite of Arthur's icy blandness.

The male Hunter spoke with authority, and apparently was used to being called a bloodsucker because he didn't complain. "We're searching for an outlaw. One of ours. I'm guessing you haven't seen any of us pass this way?"

"If I had, your search would be over, and you'd be bringing back a dead body. Well. A dead undcad body."

Rude.

75

"We're not dead, asswipe," the second Hunter protested. "That's the turned."

Knight sighed like they were boring him. "I don't give a rat's ass. Are you done? Your scent is making me feel sick."

"Let's leave this bitch to his humping." The Hunters left as quickly as they'd come. Knight didn't move off me until I couldn't smell them anymore. Once he'd slid off me and onto the floor, I pulled the sleeping bag off my face.

"Do I look undead?" I asked him moodily. I wasn't exactly pale anymore.

He chuckled at me with that gorgeous grin. "Lycan humor."

"Hilarious." I sat up and leaned closer to study his neck. My bite wasn't there anymore. All traces had already healed. Staring up at him, I realized I owed him my life. A Lycan. "Thanks for that. You umm… saved my skin."

He shrugged to seem non-committal, but I could tell he hadn't done it out of the goodness of his heart. "One last question. Did you steal that?" He pointed at the bracelet. I shook my head, and he waited a few seconds to discern if I was lying. It's not like I'd willingly have vampire teeth as a fashion accessory. "You have an Alpha's bracelet, and therefore his protection," he continued, and I remembered that the Alpha had said as much. "I'm honor bound to see that no harm comes to you. Though, I'm not in a pack, so technically I don't have to."

"You're a puddle of goodness." He flipped me off. "You're

not in a pack? Why not? No girls wanted you?" I smiled sweetly at him and he glared at me.

"You're a bit of an ass, you know that?"

"I don't know what you mean," I sassed. Standing up, I was about to start inching my way out of the cave when it occurred to me that this might be the perfect opportunity to protect Olivier. She'd never, not in a million years, predict me grouping up with a Lycan. And as a bonus, his scent seemed to mask mine from other vampires. "So..." I began timidly. I searched for the right words that wouldn't earn an automatic 'no' from him. I needed him to say yes. "Want a travel partner?" was what came out. Damn it.

He slowly brought his eyes up and stared at me like I'd just offered to give him a lap dance. Meaning he wouldn't want the lap dance, which was a shame because I gave great lap dances.

"You want to travel. With me. A Lycan." I smiled in an attempt to sell my enthusiasm at tagging along, despite the look on his face that said he thought I was two steps from insanity. I'd say maybe 1.5 steps. "No wonder your people are hunting you. They don't want a psycho around."

I wondered how fast his ribs would heal if I kicked him really hard. "For your information, *dog*, it's because-" I stopped myself and squished my lips together. If I told him the reason, he might think I was bragging or saved the pup for brownie points, or worst case scenario: lying. It didn't matter that I was on the run for what I'd done. He didn't know how our laws worked. I could be running from a pissed off ex-boyfriend for all he knew.

He studied me, trying to figure out what I was hiding, but then he gave up and looked back at the roasting rabbit. "I don't want to be around a bloodsucker. I should've killed you for feeding off me, but that bracelet protected you. So, happy trails and whatnot. Go fuck with someone else." Unphased, I walked back to the fire and sat down on the rock floor. He stared at me again and I could tell he wanted to pick me up and throw me as far as he could. "Well, you must be deaf and stupid."

I ignored him and leaned over the rabbit to smell it. The succulent scent of well-cooked meat curled into my nose. My stomach growled. "It's done. Can I have some?"

"You eat food?" he asked in sincere disbelief. His ignorance was starting to annoy me. Next he'll ask if I sleep in a coffin.

I didn't wait for permission before I extended my nails to rip off a large chunk of meat. It could've used some salt, but he'd tended it well and the meat was so juicy and tender I moaned out loud. He made a face and hogged the rest, over half the animal.

I stopped eating to study him. Despite being a Lycan, Knight looked almost normal. His muscles were large and his teeth pointed, but other than that, normal. His features were smooth and round, and they looked soft to the touch.

"Stop staring at me, crazy."

I looked down at my meat and finished it. When he was

done eating, the meat as well as the bones, he slipped into his sleeping bag and turned his back to me.

I woke up curled against his back for warmth. Oddly enough, I'd fallen asleep several feet away from him, on the other side of the fire. I cursed leaving my duffle bag in Excalibur. Now I smelled like dog. Though, admittedly, Knight didn't smell *that* bad. Then I realized what I was doing, i.e. snuggling the enemy.

But he smelled so good.

Fuck. I hurriedly pushed away from him, waking him up.

"Shit, you were actually serious," he grumbled out. I narrowly missed his swinging arm as he got up and stretched. "Bracelet or no bracelet, you're not staying here." He popped his enormous shoulders. "Don't let the cave hit your ass on the way out."

I pretended he hadn't spoken. "I have a car parked about a mile away if the Hunters haven't stolen it. There's water and snacks and blankets." He stood up and looked down at me from his enormous height, then he gestured to his large unzipped army bag, that had everything I'd just mentioned in it. "Umm. I have Twinkies?" He rolled his eyes and started gathering his stuff. "With my car, you don't have to walk! And it has air conditioning, and plenty of space for your long legs. I have long legs, and all I have to do is push the seat-"

"If I go with you, will you shut the hell up?"

"Now you're catching on!" I gave him my best smile and he sighed like I was a fly he couldn't shoo away.

Excalibur was still parked in the old barn. Knight gave it a look I might give to someone wearing Crocs, but he tossed his bag in the trunk and got in. He barely fit into the tiny passenger seat. His head bumped the roof and his legs didn't have enough space to straighten out, even with the seat pulled back as far as it could go.

"What was that you said about space for my legs?" He moved his arm and bumped me on accident.

I sighed and rested my head against the steering wheel. "Looks like our run is over, Excalibur."

He didn't comment on the name of my tiny car and didn't make any smug remarks when I had to trade it in for something else. I let him choose since I knew nothing about cars. The car he picked was a four-door Impala from the sixties, and it rumbled loudly when he started it up. I had some trepidation, but I paid for the car and got into the passenger seat (he wouldn't let me drive).

"Kind of an old car," I commented. "Will it run smoothly?"

"Old cars are like women…"

I rolled my eyes. "Are you sure you want to finish that analogy?"

He snickered. "Probably not." As he drove, he touched the steering wheel reverently and fingered the Impala symbol like it would bring him luck. We pulled out of the parking lot and drove away.

On the road, my old life at the Order seemed so far away. I leaned against my door and tried to get comfortable. Today would be companion selections. We gave the turned a companion so they could get used to being around humans again. The companions would know exactly what they were getting into, and after being chosen, they would sign a binding contract. The contract was slightly different than the one a Born companion signed. A companion of the turned had a trial period, an accident clause, and the contract lasted for one year, as opposed to the ten years of a Born companion. The turned were not in charge of their companions like we were, a fact they sometimes resented.

Knight and I didn't speak for hours. I could tell he didn't want to be traveling with me, but I had money and had bought the car, so he was tolerating it. Until I brought out my daily blood ration.

"*Shit*," he swore, and pulled the car over. "I'm not watching you drink that. That is disgusting." He turned the car off and left with the keys to walk it off. When he came back, I was finished and the blood bag was safely tucked in my cooler.

"Sorry if my dietary needs offend you," I mumbled when he started the car.

He sighed and pulled back onto the road. "I hate to sound like a judgmental parent whose kid just came out, but have you, you know, tried not drinking blood?"

What. The fuck.

I leveled him with a glare. "I'm a *vam-pi-re*," I growled,

sounding it out slowly for him. "Also, spoiler alert, I was dangerously low on blood when I attacked you. That is what happens when we don't drink blood. I don't do this shit for shiggles. Didn't they fucking teach you that in Lycan daycare? *Jesus Christ.*"

He got very quiet and focused on the road while I stewed beside him. After several hours I was almost asleep from the rhythmic sounds of the car engine, and he broke the silence, snapping me awake.

"No."

I rubbed my eye and sat up. "No what?"

"The Lycans didn't teach me that." He was very intently looking at the road to hide his face from me. "I'm sorry. I was being judgmental. I didn't understand."

"I'm sorry too." I hadn't said anything bad to him, but I'd thought several things. I supposed I was as prejudice as he was. We'd both been raised to hate the other.

Nighttime arrived and we rented a hotel room, something I hadn't dared do before now, but we could only get one with a single bed. He might've been disgusted with my species as a whole, but he was still chivalrous enough to volunteer to sleep on the floor, something I didn't expect from him at all. Maybe he was older than he looked?

He showered first and left the bathroom smelling like wet fur and a large dose of his scent. As I said, he smelled *amazing.* You know, for a Lycan. Lying in the tub surrounded by his scent, I allowed myself to forget who that smell belonged to, and I basked in the pleasure it brought. When I dressed and left the bathroom, Knight was lounging on the bed watching- wait for it- Animal Planet. He tossed back a soda, completely engrossed while dogs ran around on the screen.

I couldn't help it. I choked back a laugh.

He tossed his empty soda can in my direction. "Shut up."

I sat down in one of the chairs by the door and toweled my hair. "That dog looks pretty. I bet she's into long walks on the beach." He threw the phone book at me and I broke out into giggles.

"I'm not a dog," he said defensively, and I remembered what happened in the car.

"Sorry." Great, now I'm protecting a Lycan's feelings. "Since we're on the subject of labels, I'd prefer to not be called a bloodsucker, or any other cute slurs you can come up with."

He raked a hand through his dark hair. "Fair enough." He laid back on the bed and put a hand over his eyes. "I'm surprised you're not complaining about the dog smell. I hear that from vamps often enough." I was surprised he'd met enough of us to comment on it and was still alive. Maybe he'd lucked out and only encountered the less prejudice of us, though that was a rarity in and of itself, my own self not included.

"I didn't notice." That was a lie. I had more than noticed.

"So my smell doesn't repulse you?"

I cleared my throat and started putting on some tanning lotion. "Quite the opposite."

He raised his eyebrows at me and the corner of his mouth

quirked up. "That must've been why your scent got really intense while you were in the tub."

"*You smelled that?*" My cheeks flamed and I turned away so he wouldn't see. "I don't like being teased."

"Hey, calm down. I'm still a gentleman. Sorry I teased you." God, I needed to be more careful. His nose was better than mine. I would've never smelled someone's arousal like that. I busied myself with the lotion in the awkward silence that followed. "Hey," he said again, and I jumped to see him beside me at the giant hotel mirror. "What's with the lotion?"

I had only done one arm, so the other one was my normal pale tone. "Trying to appear more human," I told him.

"You're not as pale as I thought you'd be."

I continued rubbing the lotion in, the conversation reminding me of many discussions I'd had with my protégés. "You're thinking of the turned." Knight didn't know there were two races of vampires, and continued asking me various things on the subject. The legends only mentioned the turned, so it was normal that he didn't know about Born vampires. I figured he was beyond bored if he wanted to know so much about his natural enemies.

All of the sudden, I smelled lilac and felt a whoosh of air. Balthazar appeared in the hotel room, dressed in his normal stylish suit. When he saw Knight, he brandished his cane like a sword.

"If you are here to kill my Lisbeth, you will die before your next breath empties your lungs," he said in a dramatic tone, though I had no doubt he meant it.

"Where have you been, you little shit?" I demanded. He'd never been away from me for this long, and I was slightly miffed about it.

"Copenhagen," he replied, like it was completely obvious.

"Holy shit, where did he come from?" Knight looked slightly afraid of our visitor. Vampires that ate food he could deal with, but a being that could appear out of nowhere was apparently his limit.

Balthazar shoved his cane towards Knight and pressed it against his nose. "I reiterate the aforementioned killing should you attempt to harm my Lisbeth."

"He's cool. You can put the cane down," I told Balthazar. Well, I say cool.

He lowered it and studied my traveling companion. "You've grouped up with a wolf? And one of the marked at that. Honestly, Lisbeth, didn't I teach you better?"

I rolled my eyes. "It's not like we're doing the horizontal tango. We're just traveling together."

Knight gave me a weird look. "You use a lot of slang for a vampire."

"I like to broaden my horizons," I told him with a smile. Plus, humans tended to look at me weird when I used the word 'copulate.' I tried to keep my lingo as modern as I could.

Balthazar didn't appear to enjoy us talking to each other. "Great. Now you two are chummy."

"Yeah, I think not," I declared.

"That is so gross," was Knight's response.

"See? Even he agrees with me."

"I don't like sharing," Balthazar said as if I was his pet. "Maybe I should come with you."

"That's not happening," Knight argued firmly. "I don't even know what he is. What is he?" That was directed at me.

"An Incubus. They father vampires." I told Knight all the details, and his face shifted from confusion to outright horror. This constant explaining was making me tired. I was spoiled on people that didn't need to be told things like this. "An Incubus finds a human female, they…. Fuck, make love, whatever. She becomes pregnant, even if she was already pregnant, or barren, or dying. It doesn't matter. Nine months later, a vampire is born. A Born vampire. Like me."

Knight's caramel skin looked a little green. "Even if she's already expecting?"

Balthazar tapped his cane against his shoe and wouldn't look at us. "Yes. Even if she's already expecting."

The unasked question was there on Knight's face, and I almost wished he wouldn't ask it. He did. "What happens to the human fetus?"

"What do you think," Balthazar said quietly. He looked upset, an emotion I rarely saw on him.

Knight muttered something under his breath that sounded like, "What the fuck is this shit?"

"You okay?" I asked Balthazar. "I don't have to travel with the wolf if it really bothers you."

Thankfully, he shook his head. "No. It's safer for you to be with him. I'm simply lost in a memory. The years before you arrived were dark and empty." He disappeared without another word, leaving us slightly confused.

"Is he always like that?" Knight asked.

"Pretty much." My cheeks flushed and I remembered what we'd been discussing before Balthazar arrived. I went to bed and pulled the covers over my head.

9

WOLVES ON THE MOVE

The next morning, Knight and I sat at a diner mapping out our route across the country. His plate was loaded with enough cholesterol to stop the heart of every human in the diner. The scent of his blood called to me and my stomach was rumbling for more than just pancakes.

"I think we should route through Nevada and curve down towards Mexico before we hit Texas," he said around a mouthful of hash browns. He was still chewing when he spoke again. "If your Hunter friends are as skillful as you say, all this hopping around should throw them off."

I took a sip of my coffee and focused to drown out the scent of all the blood around me. "You eat a lot, you know that?"

His mouth curved to the side in annoyance. "I'm a wolf. My metabolism is like 50,000. If I don't eat, I fall asleep. Plus, it's not like I have a beer belly." He lifted his black shirt to expose his washboard abs. Holy mother of all that is good and right in the universe. Frozen, I sat staring at that sliver of perfection with my fork halfway to my mouth. He chuckled at me and lowered his shirt again, hiding heaven behind a curtain of fabric. "Your eyes are ginormous right now. I'm not sure how I feel about a vampire checking me out."

I coughed loudly and put the bite of food in my mouth from my suspended fork. "I was *not* checking you out, you hush your mouth. Plus you're the one who exposed yourself, so don't complain if people like what they see."

That grin appeared on his face and god, my cheeks flushed. "I thought you weren't checking me out."

"Shut *up*! I asked you not to tease me."

Still grinning, he took another bite of his food. "My apologies. It's just very entertaining to see you flustered. Your cheeks are all pink."

I pointed my fork at him. "I will steal your plate and eat all of your food, sir."

His mouth curled just a bit, and I would've laughed if I wasn't trying to be serious. "Touché, madam. Touché. I'll choose my moments carefully then. Mostly when there's no bacon involved." He looked back at the map and I pointed with my finger to another highway.

"We should make this an alternate route, just in case." He frowned and checked my face before marking it with his pen. I was leaving the option open for us to split up, and he most likely knew it. He remained silent after that, so I couldn't tell what he was thinking on the subject.

✦

After another fitful night at a roadside park, I pulled my blood bag from my cooler and squeezed a small mouthful from the plastic. Knight was watching me in-between looking at the road. The blood was heaven on my mouth, and I almost didn't want to swallow so the taste wouldn't go away. Eventually I did, and mourned the loss so much that tears came to my eyes.

I was *so* thirsty.

I put the bag back into the cooler and wiped my nose with a sniff. The bag only had about a week's worth of blood left at my current rationing, and I was drinking the barest of bare amount needed to keep me from a frenzy.

"You okay?" Knight asked when I had to wipe my cheeks. I shrugged and tried to adjust myself in my seat so I could take a nap. Sleeping was better than being awake when I was this thirsty. "We should get you another bag."

I looked at him and raised my eyebrows. "I thought drinking blood was gross to you? Why would you help me get more?"

"I'm allowed to change my opinions," he retorted moodily, and he reached a hand up to get the hair out of his eyes. "Sorry, just... Maybe I was wrong about you." Chunks of his hair fell down covering his vision again and he sighed. "Stupid hair. It's not long enough to be in a ponytail but it's long enough to be annoying." I laughed and reached in my pocket for a hair band.

"I like your hair," I commented and sat up to reach my hands towards his black locks. "Most men these days don't wear it long, or if they do, it looks scraggly." I gathered most of his hair into the hair band. It was so soft and plush, I wanted to sink my fingers into it for hours. Clearing my throat, I sat back in my seat.

"Thanks," he offered with a smile. "So about the blood thing. Maybe we could host a fake blood drive, or... Damn it."

"Still weird?" I asked him. He didn't answer for a few minutes as we pulled up next to a park. He turned the car off and played with the keys, then he looked away.

"Still weird."

My stomach growled and I told it to shut up. "I'm a tough girl. I can stick it out a little longer."

"Yeah, but," he said, and sighed. "For how long?" The question hung in the air, and he got out to grab the lunch we'd bought while I stayed in the car, motionless.

In a few more days, I could risk stealing another bag of blood and then just...suffer. Forever. Damn it. I almost started crying when I realized the truth of that thought. When would I ever have a full belly of blood again? When would the thirst stop haunting my every waking moment?

"Hey!" Knight shouted once he'd set the food up at a

picnic table. "I'm going to eat your sandwich if you don't get out."

I forced myself to open the door handle and step out of the car. I had to take this day by day. If I was constantly reminded that this was now my reality, I would break. Deep breaths. Deep. Breaths.

"Giving birth?" Knight asked me as I continued to breathe deeply on my way to the picnic table.

I wasn't in the mood for jokes. "I'm just... *really fucking thirsty.*"

"I know, I'm sorry." I sat down opposite him and noticed he'd given me one of his extra sandwiches. That broke the dam, and I started sobbing. "No, hey, it's okay. Don't do that. Ehh, tears." Something crinkled and I opened my watery eyes to see he'd given me one of his twinkies too. "No cry. I'm here to protect you, and that means blood too. We'll figure something out." Before I could respond, his nostrils flared, catching a scent I couldn't smell yet. Or just couldn't smell at all since I was weakened. He jumped up from his seat and started gathering up the food.

"What's wrong?" I looked around and saw nothing out of the ordinary.

"There's a pack coming," he said quickly, and zipped up the lunch cooler once he'd put all the food in it. "We have to leave. Right now." He stiffened again and made a growling noise in his throat. Now even I could hear a group of footsteps rapidly approaching, and in seconds, the park was flooded with a pack of about fifteen Lycans, male and female intermixed. They were all dressed like bikers in leather and old jeans. I could smell... was that blood? Animal blood, I corrected. No matter how weak I was, I could always smell fresh blood. Knight grabbed me from my seat and pushed me behind him in a protective maneuver. Normally, I would've been offended, but I was no match for all these wolves. I peeked through Knight's arm to see them, all standing in a group.

"Well, well, well," one of the wolves said in a raspy voice. His tone carried power. The Alpha male. He had dozens of tattoos up and down his arms, and looked like someone who kicked kittens for a living. "Looks like there's a wolf without a pack. Ain't that a rare sight?"

"We don't want trouble," Knight told him.

"I'm sure you don't," the Alpha said firmly. The wind changed and I could feel the pack's collective emotion shift as they caught a whiff of my smell. The mask of Knight's scent must not have fooled them. "Why are you with a soul-sucking Vampire?" *Soul-sucking.*

Growls tore from the wolves' throats and their claws clinked together as they prepared to face the threat: me. They were ready to charge at us, I didn't have to see it to know, when Knight pulled me in front of him and presented them with my arm. Specifically, the bracelet on my arm. It kept coming back to this tiny thing. The pack relaxed a little and the Alpha stared at me in absolute confusion.

"You have an Alpha's protection?" he asked me skeptically. "Why the fuck would an Alpha want to shield a vampire?"

Knight patted my shoulder. "Now would be a *perfect* time to share that. Please do." I could tell he'd been dying to ask but would've never dared to.

"I umm..." There were so many eyes staring at me. What if they judged me, even though I'd been kind to one of their pups, and ripped me to pieces right then and there? The protection of the bracelet seemed absolute, but they could just as easily treat it like a onetime pass and steal it from me. Then all bets would be off. I decided to take the risk and just tell them. "I... There was a Lycan pup that accidentally passed the Vampire border around my home." Every single Lycan in front of me had a reaction to that statement. Mistrust. Anger. Some were simply pensive, waiting for me to finish. Even Knight's hand tensed on my shoulder. "I might be a Vampire, and my hands have taken lives. But I don't kill children. Not even pups."

The Alpha was still regarding me, trying to figure me out. "You let him go. You spared him."

"Yes." There was no need to embellish what I'd done.

The Alpha stepped towards us and gestured to Knight. "Is it his bracelet?" I shook my head. Did it matter? "It's an ancient tradition among us that the one who holds the bracelet of an Alpha is under his protection. No one really knows where it came from, but it's generally understood that the Alpha who gifted the bracelet is who protects the one wearing it." He looked up at Knight. "You're an Alpha," he stated, not even asking. "It's not obvious at the first glance, but shit, there's something off with you." So I wasn't the only one who'd noticed something off about Knight. While I'd never have guessed he was an Alpha, it wasn't much of a stretch. Kind of made him more adorable.

Shut up, brain.

"She's under my protection now, since her Alpha isn't here," Knight told him. Well. That explained why he'd let me tag along with him. Though, since I held the money, technically he was tagging along with me.

The Alpha's mate walked up to stand beside him. "He's an Alpha, Jesse?" She made a noise like she was having a hard time believing it, and then she got serious. "Ah. I can see it now. Where's your bracelet, Alpha?"

"I don't have one," Knight responded.

Well fuck. Even I was shocked. From what I could tell about the bracelets, they were a symbol of status, showing everyone who could see that you and your pack were strong enough to slay Vampires. The Alpha of this pack had at least thirty fangs on his bracelet whereas mine only had about ten. Talk about a virtual penis. Knight might not be in a pack, but he was almost twice as big as the Alpha in front of us. Of course, I'd never seen Knight wearing a fang bracelet, but I just assumed he kept it hidden since he didn't have a pack to back up his claim of strength. I turned around and looked up at him, suddenly only thinking of one thing to ask him.

"Why not?"

He glanced down at me and said simply, "I've never killed a vampire."

Oh.

"A Lycan that doesn't kill Vampires and a Vampire that spares Lycans," the Alpha, Jesse, said with a chuckle. "What a fucking pair."

"I'm not sure he's a Lycan," the Alpha female said suddenly. She'd been studying Knight for several minutes, apparently noticing things that I hadn't. Not a Lycan? Of course he was a Lycan! What else would he be? A hippo? "I'd call him a werewolf, but that would be impossible."

The fuck?

"Aren't they... you... the same thing?" I asked her. Apparently, it was the wrong question to ask because they both got offended.

"What the fuck, it is *not* the same thing! Werewolves turn with the full moon," the Alpha female said with a haughty sniff. "They're wild and uncontrollable when they shift."

I felt Knight grow rigid as they talked. The Alpha female dismissed her observation as a random thought and dropped it, but she kept eyeing Knight with suspicion. We left the pack after they shared some barbecued deer with us and Jesse gave us his number with the promise they'd help us if we needed it. I suspected the offer was more for Knight than me.

When we were miles away, I opened my mouth to ask Knight about what the Alpha female had said, but he quickly turned the radio on full blast to drown me out. So, he was okay with protecting me, but not okay with me asking about how everyone kept mentioning that there was something weird about him. Whether or not he felt like sharing whatever he was hiding, if what the Alpha female said was true, he only had a few days until the next full moon. If I royally pissed him off and he didn't shift, I'd have my answer.

Balthazar had referred to Knight as 'the marked', and now Knight had been called a 'werewolf' instead of a Lycan. What the hell was he?

When we reached the border of Texas, I was instantly hit with the scent of pack territory, the fragrant smell of warm piss. *Oh god, why?*

Knight started fiddling with his keys to distract himself from growling out of instinct. We continued until the smell was gone and checked into a fancy hotel for the night. Staying at only fleabag hotels was a pattern and easily tracked, so we went off the trail every so often and stayed at very expensive hotels. That night, we had our own beds in a two-room suite, room service, and a large pool to swim in.

Knight left to go swimming as soon as we put our stuff in the suite. I drank the last few droplets from my bag of blood. It was now empty. I set it on fire in one of the trash bins until it was ash, and then flushed the ashes down the toilet. My hand shook and I clenched it into a fist. I'd be okay. I'd figure this out.

Being alone in my room was only going to make me feel weaker, so I put on the denim jacket I'd bought in Chicago and walked down to the pool. The humans had all gone to bed, leaving Knight alone in the water swimming laps. I sat down on one of the pool chairs and hugged myself tightly against my cold body to watch him. I had no doubt that he knew I was there, but he didn't stop.

Now that I was seeing him shirtless, I could see his body had more muscle mass than I'd originally thought from that small glimpse of his abs. And yeah, it was much hotter than it sounds. He looked like a carved sculpture, designed for my viewing pleasure. I mean, human females. Not me, a vampire.

Diving under, he resurfaced and stood up in the shallow pool, the water only coming up to his sternum and revealing a very small patch of black chest hair. His rippled chest was decorated with five long scratches that looked pink like he'd gotten them recently, but I could tell they had been there awhile. He ran his hands through his thick black hair to get it out of his face, and then he noticed me sitting there watching him.

"Do you always peep on your friends?" I watched a drop of water go from his neck, down his chest, and flutter along his abs before stopping at the waistband of his swimming trunks. I wished I was that drop of water.

No, stop it! Focus!

"You want to come in here with me?" Blinking, I looked away from the way his trunks were sticking to his body and found his face. He smiled at me, making my heart flutter inside my chest.

"I don't umm…" I cleared my throat, trying to look anywhere except right into his eyes. "I don't think that would be appropriate. I don't have a bathing suit."

He shrugged and his grin taunted me. "That's never stopped me before."

Oh, you are a bad man.

He noticed me hugging myself. "Why are you wearing a jacket? This is Texas. It's not cold."

I took it off and smiled disarmingly. "I'm used to living in New York State. It's not as warm there. Habit, I guess."

He studied me for a few seconds but didn't press me further. "Sure you won't come in? I promise to behave. The water is nice. I know it's cliché to be a wolf and like water," he added with a roll of his eyes. I laughed and tried not to shiver. The lack of blood was making my body temperature fall. If anyone touched me, my skin would be cold. Because of that, the thought of swimming in cold water wasn't appealing to me, as much as I would've enjoyed it under normal circumstances. He must've sensed my suffering because Knight stopped smiling and got out of the pool. He walked over to me, leaving puddles of water and large foot-prints. "You need blood," he stated when he stood in front of me. He didn't have to ask.

"I'm fine," I lied, my teeth chattering a few times. He picked my jacket up and draped it over my shoulders, then he slumped down in the pool chair next to me.

"Being with you is…." I waited for him to finish his sentence. Damn it, was this his leaving speech? "…hard." I let out the air I'd been holding. I didn't feel like having this conversation so low on blood. When I tried to get up, he grabbed my arm and sat me back down. "Being around a vampire is like a priest living with Rosemary's baby. Your habits, drinking blood, I can't stand them. When I was a boy, we were taught that vampires drank because they were monsters. No one said anything about you needing it to stay strong, and live. I'll admit, it's not your average diet, but…" He raked his hands through his hair again. "It's clear you can't survive without it, even though you're trying to. And again, I'm sorry for what I said about that." I tried to speak, but I was too cold. So cold. Icicle Lisbeth. Maybe I'd turn into a gorgeous ice statue and Knight would come to admire me on Tuesdays. "Come here," he beckoned and patted his knee. I stared down at it like it was a grenade. No, I couldn't let him touch me. My attraction for him was something I wasn't supposed to feel. He clicked his tongue, stood up, and grabbed me. Even shirtless, he was so *fucking* warm. Any trepidation I'd had was out the window and I buried my face in his chest, pulled him closer to me as much as possible. "You weren't freezing the last time," he noted and held me so tightly with his thick arms.

"S-s-side effects v-v-vary every-t-t-time," I chattered out and moaned against him. "You're so *warm*."

"Shit," he swore, and his hands curled against my shirt. "Here, let me help." He let me go before I could ask what he meant. I needed his warmth so badly, my hands reached out for him without thinking, and I looked up into his deep brown eyes to see what was wrong. Slowly, his right hand came up to slide across my cheek where he held my chin in place. His other hand smoothed my long curls out of my face and knotted amongst their length.

He leaned into me and stopped with his mouth inches from mine, stroking my chin in a soft dance. My breath came in ragged bursts, my body was in flames from his touch. And though this was only my first time being this close to him, I needed more. I hungered for this Lycan's touch like I'd never wanted anyone's before. But *why*, for the love of god? He was a Lycan, for fuck's sake. I shouldn't be this attracted to him.

Those lips just inches from mine whispered, "Are you still cold?"

I had no concept of cold with a furnace of passion standing in front of me. I shook my head, and he was gone before I could blink.

Mother fucker.

His bitch ass was halfway down the sidewalk to our room when I opened my eyes. I followed him away from the pool into the hotel, and he was already in his room with the door shut by the time I got there. With our perfect hearing and the rooms so close, we could hear everything the other was doing. If he started jerking off, I'd hear it.

Why had he done that? Was he teasing me again? Teasing was the worst. No, jack ass, I was certainly not cold anymore. Now I was burning internally from his touch, and I hated myself for it. After I fluffed my pillows five times, Knight sighed and started talking to me from the other room.

"How old did you say you were?"

I adjusted my hair against the pillow. My skin was still overheated from his touch. Damn him. "Don't you know it's not polite to ask a lady how old she is?"

"Fine. Just tell me the century."

"16th."

He paused, and I couldn't tell if he was impressed or about to make a joke. "Okay then. What was life like... you know... four hundred years ago?"

"You're probably expecting me to say something like it smelled terrible."

"Probably."

"It actually smelled like shit had died and gone to heaven, and then was reincarnated as shit again. But beyond that, it was also hard. Life was hard. Not just simple things like washing a shirt or plucking a pheasant. Living was so *damn* hard. There were no guarantees about anything. You could go to bed and wake up to the news that five of your friends had gotten sick and died. Or they were victims of robbers. Or the king had ordered a village slaughtered because he fucking felt like it." I swiped my eyes to catch some tears. "We were more connected with the humans in those days. Their fragility was always around us, staring us in the face. That's why we keep to ourselves now. It's easier that way.

Plus, some of us have superiority complexes. Present company excluded."

I was trying to make him laugh, but Knight was silent for a long time. When I'd convinced myself he'd fallen asleep, he suddenly sighed and said, "Since we're sharing, I should tell you something."

"Okay?"

"I was born over a hundred years ago."

10

THE IMMORTAL WOLF

*W*hat. The shit.

"Okay. I think my brain just went for a walk. You said what now?"

"I'm not repeating it," he insisted grumpily.

"Is that umm… normal for Lycans?" As much as I wanted to sound smart, I really had no idea if it was or not. "Or are you just a weirdo as I suspected you are?"

"You're not being very reassuring considering you're the only person I've ever told."

I was about to ask him more when he opened the door between our rooms and walked in wearing pajama bottoms, carrying pillows and a comforter.

I pulled my blanket up to cover my chest, even though I wasn't the one who was topless. I could be, easily. "Uh…. what's up?"

"Your scent gets stronger when I'm too far away," he said simply, and deposited his pallet on my floor.

"You're in a lady's bedchamber," I told him. He lifted an eyebrow at me, silently reminding me we'd been sharing a room for a while now, not to mention what had happened at the pool, and continued adjusting his comforter.

When he laid down, he said in a sarcastic tone, "I'll try not to pleasure you in my sleep."

Disappointing.

The next day we traveled through a town that grew fruit, so we decided to stop early and get a room at a bed and breakfast. We'd been traveling together for about two weeks, and I'd been running for even longer, so it was time for a tiny break. The bed and breakfast we'd decided on was part of a peach orchard. Fruit trees dotted the acreage around the old white house, most of them peach, but several were apricot and plum. As part of our room deal, we could pick a bushel of fruit to take with us.

Knight picked the fruit expertly, knowing which were ripe, too ripe, and not ripe enough. He could reach the branches without a ladder, so I stood next to him with the bushel. His face was so excited, it was becoming contagious. After placing another fruit in the basket with an enormous grin on his face, I gave him a questioning look.

"I didn't realize you loved fruit this much Mr. I'll-take-the-largest-fucking-burger-you-have." I'd never seen him eat vegetation that wasn't between sesame seed buns or deep fried in oil.

He shoved me playfully and almost made me drop the basket. "I grew up on an orchard, almost exactly like this one, in fact. It was before the war." By war, he meant the Civil War. "The trees were so stunning in the spring. Pink peach blossoms are the most beautiful flowers I've ever seen. It made me wish I could paint them just to capture their beauty." He gave a mournful grin and tossed another peach into the bushel. "That was a long time ago. I came back after the war to run the orchard with my mother, but a plague of locusts came. Those fuckers ate everything green and beautiful. Then when everything green was gone, they chewed the wood on the house, the clothes we left out to dry, the rope on the fences. It was a shit storm." He sat down and played with the peach in his hands. I could easily picture him over a hundred years ago, seeing everything he'd ever loved being destroyed.

"I was in Japan around then," I said quietly. "We had to escape in case anyone found our castle during the war, so we all went to different countries. They have cherry trees in Japan. Have you ever seen one?" He shook his head, still lost in the past. I started picking peaches from the lower branches and had to use a step stool.

"Sorry," he said after several minutes of me struggling to reach the fruit. I usually wore heels to make me taller, since I was only average height, but right now I was sticking to hipster sneakers and sandals.

"Sorry for telling me all that or sorry you're cruelly reminding me that you're over a foot taller than I am?" He laughed then and the past was gone from his face. "A little help?" I asked him and pointed to some peaches I couldn't reach.

"You're doing fine," he answered with a mischievous grin.

"Ass." I threw a peach at him, but I should've known better because he started a fruit fight with the bruised peaches that lay on the ground. I wasn't that good of a throw since I wasn't at top strength, but I held my own. Hiding behind a tree, I picked up a few peaches to throw and searched for him. I couldn't see him, and I couldn't risk using energy to push my senses out. My sense of smell was very limited this low on blood. "Stop hiding, butthole," I shouted. "You know I can't smell you right now." He dropped down from the peach tree and I screamed, dropping the fruit onto the ground while he laughed at me. "*Asshole!*"

The sight of him laughing took my breath away, and I didn't stop him when he leaned in and pressed my back against the peach tree. The sticky bark was rough under my hands, my nails dug into the wood when Knight reached up to pull a twig from my hair.

Would he kiss me? Of course he wouldn't. He said he found me repulsive, and rightly so. "That is so gross," he'd said. Those four words repeated in my head until I had to look away from his gaze.

107

"What's wrong?" he asked, studying me so closely, I felt my knees wobble. You're a tease, that's what's wrong. And I shouldn't have been attracted to you, but I was.

"We should get back," I answered, looking away.

He nodded and stepped away from me. I started towards the bed and breakfast with him beside me, both of us silent. Our mood was further killed as we came closer and saw a police car sitting in front of the house. Knight took my hand and we scurried behind a shed where we wouldn't be seen. The local sheriff was talking to the owner of the bed and breakfast, who gestured to the Impala and then the window of our room.

He was here for me.

Knight tugged on my hand, making my stomach flip over, and put a finger to his lips, then gestured he was going to get our bags from the room and I needed to stay here. He left, and though I knew it would use up most of the blood I had left, I pushed my senses out to listen in on the sheriff and the proprietor. It was extremely difficult, but I managed to keep it up for a few minutes.

"...so she didn't look suspicious?"

"No! I can't believe she killed a little girl!" What? What was she talking about?

"What about the man with her?"

"He was... well, he's a big man, but he wasn't rude. Just being near him was enough to make you piss yourself." I tried not to laugh. Knight was extremely intimidating, with just his height alone. Good thing he hadn't flashed his pointed teeth. Ooo. I'd like to see that.

"He must be an accomplice," the sheriff concluded, unfairly.

I gasped as my senses pulled back in. I felt even weaker now. Knight was there before I noticed he was near, carrying our bags over his shoulder. He took my hand again and said one word:

"Run."

A month ago, running would've been so easy and so much fun, but weeks of drinking bagged blood had turned me into an invalid. Only a blood frenzy would strengthen me now, or just, you know, drinking from someone. I wasn't even sure a frenzy would work at this point. So, when Knight grabbed me and told me to run, I failed miserably. I ran for about two minutes, but then my legs stopped working properly and I started tripping over my own feet.

"God damn it," he cursed, and then he adjusted the bags, picked me up, and kept running. With my legs wrapped around his waist and his arms holding me against his chest, my mouth was right on his neck. His warm skin was an invitation, not just to drink, but to indulge the feeling building inside me at being so close to him, just for a few minutes.

Knight ran across the Texan countryside for over an hour, not slowing and not even winded. Every minute or so he adjusted his hands on me to make sure I was still there and not falling off him. My arms were too weak to even anchor myself on his neck. He finally slowed down and stopped for a few minutes to rest, though from the way he was breathing, you'd never have known he'd just run that far carrying a vampire and two bags.

He sighed like he was about to speak, and I stilled, waiting for him to complain or maybe grab my ass. "My car," was all he said. I giggled and he laughed too, the movement shaking my head.

"Call Jesse, he'll keep it for you." The Alpha had said to call him if we needed anything. This was anything.

"Text him," Knight said to me. "Where's the phone?"

I dropped my head against his shoulder. "I don't think I can make my hand hold it."

He rubbed my back to soothe me, holding me closer to keep me from falling. He was so nice to me, and he had no reason to be. "Just wait a little longer." We were off again, Knight navigating the terrain like a pro until we'd been gone for several hours. The sun was setting when he stopped again. I vaguely registered the sound of him stepping into a pool of warm water, and then he set me down on the stone floor of a cave. Behind him was a waterfall, and we were slightly hidden in the curtain of water. He sat down at my feet and we both rested. The water was a natural hot spring, the steam of it made the cave air warm.

After a few minutes, he glanced over at me. "I think your lotion is all rubbed off." I certainly felt pale, so I was probably a lot whiter than normal. I started sliding down the wall

ELIZABETH DUNLAP

since I couldn't hold myself up, but Knight was there to catch me.

I let him guide me onto his lap, I was kind of powerless to do otherwise, but when he tilted his head to the side to expose his neck, I froze. "What are you doing?" I asked him with trepidation, though I knew full well what he was offering. A small part hoped he wasn't just offering blood.

"I heard the humans back there. Your kind has involved their law enforcement to find you. The hospitals will probably be on alert as well. Stealing blood was already risky. Now it'll give us away." He swallowed, met my eyes, and his hand came up to grip my arm. "I'm offering this willingly. I told Jesse I would protect you, and I meant it. Now drink before I change my mind."

My fangs almost hurt from lack of use as they slid down. I didn't need them when I drank bagged blood, so they'd been pushed up for weeks. With them down, my senses opened slightly and Knight's scent washed over me, and it was so amazing, I could've wept, but he also smelled different. I couldn't put my finger on it.

He put his hands on my waist, so I leaned in and gasped when my teeth sunk into him. I think he moaned, but I didn't notice. All I could focus on was his blood. It tasted so good. It was like almost dying and feeling life pour into you again, which wasn't far from the truth considering how weak I'd been. I drank deeply and freely. I was surprised I wasn't draining him. Normally, my companion stopped me when they started to feel weak, but Knight let me go as long as I wanted to. As soon as I felt stronger, I restrained myself and pulled away. Knight's hands were fisted in my shirt, so I stayed still until he relaxed. As I watched, his neck started to heal until my bite marks were gone, as if they'd never happened.

Timidly, I put my arms around his neck and held him close. He owed me that. "I drank too much." If I weakened him, we wouldn't survive.

"No, you didn't." His voice was muffled by my shirt. "My body will make new blood, so always drink however much you need." Always? I tried not to read too much into his choice of words. "Move that ass, I need some water." I stood and found a spot against the cave wall to watch him take a drink from one of our bottles of water. I shivered, but I was the furthest thing from chilly. He looked over at me and noticed. "Are you cold?"

"Yes," I said breathlessly. Getting enough air was hard with my teeth starting to chatter.

"Let's go for a swim."

Yes, please.

He reached a hand out and when our fingers touched, I felt a jolt of electricity go up my arm. So warm. He was so warm. He led me down to the hot springs and slowly the warm water chased away all the ice. Or maybe it was holding his hand. I couldn't say.

Once we were in the middle of the pool, the water came up to my armpits. Knight dunked his head and resurfaced, shaking his head to get the water out of his eyes. Water droplets sprayed on me and I yelped to get away, then dunked my own head underwater so it won't matter. He laughed and went below the surface again, only to come back up right in front of me. I stumbled backward and he caught me with a hand around my waist.

"I have a question for you," he began, his breath coming in visible bursts. The hand on my waist pulled me closer to him, so close his foggy breath was on my face. I was very certain I wouldn't be able to articulate an answer to whatever he wanted to know. "If I hadn't promised to protect you..." His other hand came up to wipe a bead of moisture off my bottom lip. "Would you still want me to be with you?"

"I uhh..." I swallowed and tried not to focus on his eyes, or his lips. "I have a question for you."

A crinkled formed between his eyes. "Okay."

"How can you be this close to me if I repulse you?"

Something in his face changed, an edge of sadness, of disappointment, and I felt like a fool for ruining whatever he'd been trying to do.

"We don't have long," he said, trying to move his hands away from me. His body had gone rigid. What had I done?

"No, don't." I stopped his hands with my own and held them around my waist. "Why don't we have long?"

"Lisbeth," Knight breathed in warning. I was so distracted I almost didn't hear the inflections in his voice. His hands started crushing into my hips and it was hurting me.

"Knight, what's wrong?" I asked him, reaching a hand up

to his face. Over his shoulder, I saw the clouds part and the moon came out.

Let me say that again. The full moon came out.

The moonlight hit Knight like it was searching for him, and his body stiffened in response. His eyes were usually dark brown, but now they were glowing bright yellow. He met my gaze, and I'd never seen so much terror in someone's eyes before. I took a step back from him, all the heat gone from my body and replaced with white cold fear.

Under the moon's grasp, Knight started shifting. His hands lengthened into long claws, his muscles grew even bigger, and his face contorted into a snout. Hair sprouted on his body, so where he used to be mostly hairless, he now had black wispy curls. His scent turned acrid and almost made me choke because I was standing so close to him.

When he was fully shifted, he looked like a wolf-human hybrid, not the dog-like wolf I'd expected. That's when I knew the Alpha female was right.

Knight wasn't a Lycan. He was a werewolf.

The werewolf with Knight's eyes growled low in his chest and threw his head back to howl at the moon. My ears rang at the sound.

"Knight, are you okay?" I stepped close to check on him, but it was a mistake.

This creature wasn't Knight anymore. While the moon held him in her grasp, Knight was gone, and what had taken his place was a bi-pedal wolf that saw me as its mortal enemy. He swung his arm at me so quickly, I couldn't move away fast enough, and he sliced my stomach open with his enormous claws. The werewolf's other hand came up and broke my neck in a swift punch.

Then he howled at his precious moon again, and left his enemy to bleed out and die.

11

ON THE PROWL FOR BLOOD

I woke up several hours later, floating in the pool of water. My wounds had healed and my neck wasn't broken anymore, but it had used up most of the blood I'd gotten from Knight to repair what he'd done to me. Thankfully, I had enough strength left to push my senses out and see where I was. Knight had been overly cautious, it seemed, as our campsite was far from the nearest town. I hobbled back to the cave and put some clothes on.

Fucking fantastic. This was how he treated girls. He holds them close and then breaks their necks. Not my idea of romance, but maybe that's just me. Sure, he looked like he wanted to kiss me, but in the end, I was still his enemy. I was so fucking stupid. He'd never want me, not ever. I couldn't believe I'd trusted a werewolf.

Once I was dry, I ate dinner and curled up in his blanket to fall asleep.

When morning came, Knight wasn't there. Waiting all day did no good. He didn't come back. After the third day of sitting in the cave, literally dying of thirst, I got up and shouldered my bag, leaving Knight's things in the cave. I couldn't survive without blood, and if he wanted to find me he could. I walked the long distance to the human town and couldn't help but notice how lonely and quiet it was.

Lonely and quiet without him.

The town was small enough that my picture wasn't being circulated, and no one was talking about me killing an innocent child (I was still pissed about that). Knight's scent wasn't around, so I tried to relax. Darkness was already falling, the last night of the full moon, and while this town was very small, it had one redeeming factor: a nightclub.

I found a used clothing store still open and bought something that reminded me of Olivier: a black leather dress with pockets and a million zippers. To go with it, I found some clunky black boots decorated with belt buckles. The cashier looked at me weird since I was dressed like a beach girl and buying gothic clothes. I changed in an alley and stashed my bag beside a dumpster after arranging my hair in messy curls and applying some makeup from my purse.

The vampire was feeding tonight.

I channeled my sensual side as I walked up to the club. The heavy closed doors held in loud pounding music that oozed from the large warehouse. The sound was muffled to those on the street, but for me, it was like I was already inside. I passed the waiting line of teenagers with fake I.D.'s and went right up to the bouncer.

It should be noted that I'd never actually been to a club, so I was acting out what I'd seen on television. The hot girls always kiss up to the club bouncer, and if he's straight, he lets them in ahead of everyone else.

My heels clicked on the pavement until I stopped at the front door. The bouncer was stacked with muscles and looked like that guy from the racing movies Cameron liked to watch. Knight's muscles were just as impressive. I smiled sweetly and waved at the bouncer when he noticed me. His eyes swept my body and I could tell he liked what he saw, but apparently it wasn't enough to get me in the club.

"Back of the line with that sweet ass, baby."

Seriously? Okay, what would Olivier do? That was easy: she'd deck him and use his body as a rug to walk into the club. I racked my brain for an idea.

What would Knight do?

I didn't even have to guess that answer. I opened my purse and pulled out several hundred dollar bills, and then I waved them in the bouncer's face. "How's three hundred bucks sound?"

He swiped them from me and slid the bills into his pocket. "Enjoy the club, baby." He motioned and the big guy at the entrance opened one of the doors for me. If I'd thought the music was slightly loud outside, the music inside was deafening. I stepped into the large room packed with sweaty dancing humans.

My prey.

I recoiled at the thought. Humans weren't considered prey anymore, but to rogue vampires like me, I suppose they were. Oh yeah, I guess I was a rogue vampire now. That sounded mysterious and sexy.

I forced myself to focus. The room stunk of sweat and pheromones. Anger, passion, jealously. Music poured through the speaker system, and it wasn't a bad tune so I had to keep myself from swaying to it as I herded through the crowd of people to get a drink.

The club was lit by strobe lights that moved and bobbed with the beat of the music like someone was controlling them. Smoke machines poured out steam around the dance floor, making the dancers look ethereal and haunting as they swayed in a hypnotic dance.

When I got to the bar, I ordered a Bloody Mary and leaned against the LED lit counter to watch the humans dance. I'd started thinking of ways to feed that were discreet when my nose smelled lilac. I turned, and standing one inch away from my face was Balthazar dressed in black leather pants, a white shirt, and a black leather vest.

He always had to look so fucking delicious.

I had to lean in close to his ear for him to hear me over the noise. "You've been wearing the same suit for 120 years, but you should wear those leather pants more often. Can I see your ass in those? I need that memory for later."

He gave me a dry smile and searched around me for someone. "Where's the dog?"

I shrugged and sipped my drink. "He bailed." The words, or the drink, left a bad taste in my mouth.

"Good. You smell like him. It stinks."

"I do not stink!" I smacked his arm and he laughed, showing all of his perfect teeth and accidentally drawing the attention of every girl around us. Balthazar noticed for once, and dropped his smile so the females would leave him alone. Not that it worked, since they were now gathering in small groups around the bar to watch the sex god standing next to me.

He ordered a pink martini and leaned against the bar, pretending to be oblivious to the humans staring at him. "Did you make love to him?"

I almost spit my drink out. "What. The fuck," I coughed.

Taking a sip of his drink, he looked at me from over the rim. "I said you smelled like him. I failed to mention *where* you smelled like him."

"You are…." I downed my drink in one go and ordered another.

"You're low on blood. Interesting hunting ground, this." He gestured with his drink at the dancing humans.

"It's not like I have options," I told him. He shrugged so we sipped our drinks and surveyed the masses on the dance floor. I spotted a skinny boy wearing tight jeans and a striped shirt. His scent wasn't too bad, so I left Balthazar at the bar to approach my target. The lights in the club were so dim that the humans wouldn't be able to see me do some sleight of hand, so long as one of the strobes didn't hit me.

I was two seconds away from discreetly slicing the boys arm and filling my glass with his blood, but I stopped suddenly as Knight's face came to me, and everything we'd shared, as weird as it all had been. He thought I was a monster for drinking blood. Maybe I was if I did it like this. This wasn't right. I couldn't drink without someone's consent. It went against everything I stood for. I almost wished I was hungry enough for a frenzy. At least in that state, I didn't have the option of asking first and biting later.

Balthazar didn't comment when I stomped back to him and slammed my empty goblet onto the bar. It shattered from the force of my vampire strength.

"Damn it," I swore as the shards tore into my skin. I couldn't afford to waste precious blood. I left the club with Balthazar behind me. We walked to the alley where my bag was and I started picking the glass out of my hand.

If anyone else had been standing there with me, I would've expected a lecture, or at least pelting me with questions, but Balthazar wasn't like that. "I suppose you're raiding a hospital now?" he asked me quietly after my hand had healed. I groaned at the thought of bagged blood, but if I wanted to keep my morals, it was the only option open to me. Balthazar produced a small wrapped box from nowhere and held it out to me. "I got you this. Happy Hallows Eve."

"It's September." He shook the box in my face so I'd take it. Inside was a familiar set of car keys. Stunned, I started to ask him why, not to mention how, he had them, but he put his hand up and gestured for me to follow him. Sitting in the parking lot across the street was Excalibur, safe and sound.

I couldn't think of a response beyond hugging his arm, which I did. "I'm impressed," I told him with a smile. How he'd managed to find and buy my car back was beyond me. Though, if it had belonged to a female, I doubted he had to pay anything for it.

"You're on your own now, you need to take care of yourself," he said. "I would've helped before but I was busy."

"Busy with some ladies in Copenhagen?" I joked.

He rolled his eyes, grinning down at me. "Wouldn't you like to know?"

"I would actually. With details."

He kissed me on the cheek, and then he disappeared.

When I sat inside my little fuel efficient car, it felt like I'd never left. I sat there for a few minutes, waiting for something, and I realized I'd been waiting for Knight to open the passenger door and sit next to me. But he was gone, and I was still alone.

Damn him. I had to erase him from my mind and continue on my path. I drove Excalibur for an hour before I pulled over and started planning my next activity: robbing a hospital. It seemed simple enough. If I found a small one, maybe they wouldn't be on alert about someone stealing blood and Arthur wouldn't find out. Maybe. I was doubtful on that account, but if I waited any longer, I'd go into a frenzy and then it would all be over. Arthur would find me, no question about it. And then no more running, no more friends, no more me. No more... Knight.

No, stop thinking about him. I wasn't going to let four hundred plus years go to waste, werewolf or no werewolf.

One crappy hotel room, a large order of Japanese take away, and a case of soda later, I had a solid enough plan put together. I rolled up the paper I'd written my game plan on and started picking up the take away trash when my phone rang. I'd considered buying a new burner phone since Renard had called me and the number could be traced if Arthur felt like doing so, but the thought of someone at the castle needing me and not being able to find me, mainly Olivier or Cameron, kept me from doing so. Plus, I'd given my number to Knight as well. I picked the phone up and saw 'Unregistered number' on the screen.

I pressed the answer button, having no idea who was calling me. "Hello?" I waited for Arthur's deep scratchy voice, but it was someone else.

"Hey."

My throat constricted as I heard Knight's voice on the other end. I searched for something to say since the only thing I wanted to ask him was where he was. If he was okay. If he missed me. "I umm... I'm not dead."

"Yeah... I noticed." I sat in awkward silence for a few minutes before he cleared his throat. "Have you fed?"

Why would he ask me that? "No." I wanted to tell him about the club, but I felt embarrassed at what I'd almost done. "I'm going to raid a hospital."

"Can't that Incubus help? You know, steal it for you?"

"I can take care of myself, thank you."

"Makes sure you're okay but leaves you high and dry? What a friend."

I scowled and felt my nails lengthen. "At least he doesn't attack me and leave me for dead in a pool of water. If that's your idea of foreplay, I'm not into it."

Knight made a grumbling noise under his breath. "Right. Because I always have complete control when I shift. Can't believe I fucking forgot to mention that." He sighed loudly. "This isn't why I called you. I just want to make sure you're eating."

More like make sure I'm not snacking on innocent people for fun. "I'll have blood before the sun rises."

"Fine." The line abruptly cut off.

12

AN UNEXPECTED DISCOVERY

*A*fter an hour of blaring the car radio so I wouldn't have to think about that *buttfaced werewolf*, I arrived at the hospital.

The parking lot was quiet when I approached, and most of the hospital lights were turned off. The town around it was equally silent, something you wouldn't find in a larger city, which was perfect for me. It was very late at night, and that meant pretending to visit a patient was out of the question. I'd opted for a more secret agent spy approach. I entered the hospital through the emergency room door and slipped out of the ER waiting room down an empty hallway. I push my senses out to examine the rooms around me until I found the scent of hospital scrubs. I followed the smell to a hall closet that had spare doctor robes and blue nurse scrubs. The nurse scrubs were the last thing I'd ever want to be seen wearing, but I swallowed my fashion sense and put a set on over my clothes.

My next move was tricky. This was a small hospital in a small town and I had no doubt that everyone knew everyone else, or at least remembered faces well enough to know that my face hadn't been there before. It was unfortunate that I hadn't drunk several times that day or I'd be able to manipulate my way to the blood bank. Since I was a rogue vampire now, what was another law broken? Luckily, the doors I needed to pass through were either unlocked or locked from the opposite side, so I didn't need to steal anyone's keycard. I made my way to the stairs after checking a hospital map for the location of the blood bank.

Lack of blood was making my head pound, and it was only getting worse. I was dangerously close to a frenzy. My senses were so closed in that I could barely smell the humans even when they stood nearby me. I stumbled on the stairs and over my own feet several times before I got to the right floor. Move, legs. Don't fail me when I'm so close. The orders to my legs did no good, forcing me to hug the wall slightly to stay upright.

As I got to the blood bank, I was greeted with a locked door. I smacked my head on the door a few times and wondered why I thought I could even get away with this. Espionage wasn't my thing, a fact I had just proved. Of course, the door would be locked. Why would it not be? I groaned and beat my head against the door again. Black was coming into my vision. I was so close to the edge.

"Need something?" Startled, I whirled around and leaned back on the door when my equilibrium failed me. Standing two feet away was a handsome Indian man wearing typical doctor scrubs with a white coat over them. "Oh my," he said in slightly accented English. "You look quite close to the edge." What was he talking about? Maybe he thought I was high on drugs. I thought about playing it up, but I hadn't been playing before now and he was already convinced I was a stoner. "What you need isn't in there, my friend. Come with me."

He held out a hand to me, and I saw no reason to not take it. Once he took me somewhere and we were alone, I'd just bite him and pretend he agreed to it. Knight could shove it up his hairy ass.

"We don't have time, let's go." The doctor gripped my hand tightly and put his other one around me to tote me along. He was surprisingly strong for a human. He half carried me to a nurse's station on the other side of the floor. Two women were sitting in chairs eating popcorn, and I couldn't even smell it. They got up when we arrived and started fussing over getting me to a chair. "She needs a gift," he told them.

I was about to ask what the fuck he was talking about when one of the nurses unbuttoned her collar and pulled it aside to reveal her neck. There was no time to ponder what was going on, why a human was offering her blood to me so willingly, why she knew that I needed it, or who these people were and if they'd turn me into Arthur.

I dove for her neck and sank my teeth in, and her blood flooded into my mouth like water in a desert.

A hand slipped around my neck, the Doctor's, no doubt monitoring how much I took and ready to rip me off if I drank too much. As soon as the first mouthful slipped down my throat, I regained control and pulled away when I could tell the nurse had given almost too much. Her blood had a weird flavor, almost like I'd been feeding from an animal instead of a human. It sustained me, but it left a bad taste in my mouth. I'd have to brush my teeth later.

"You are Born," the doctor remarked as I used a tissue to wipe my mouth. "I wasn't sure at first, you were so pale, so like the dead. But there it is, the color is returning to you." His stance had changed from cautious to relaxed since now he knew I wouldn't attack the humans. "My name is Ahmed." The nurse's blood raced through my system and I could suddenly feel his essence. He was old, slightly older than me. I hadn't noticed, so low on blood, that he was also a vampire.

"Lisbeth," I said back.

He nodded and appraised me for a moment before moving back to the hall. "Come, I will show you the city." At this point, it was too late to run if they were going to tell Arthur about me. I might as well stay. We left the nurses and walked down the hallway. "That was quite a bit of espionage to get into the hospital." He turned his head to look back at me and smiled. "But you were so far gone, your eyes were turning black. Another second and I would've had to kill you." He said it casually, like killing me was the same as getting me coffee. What a kidder.

I'd almost forgotten what being around my kind was like. More so, those of my kind that didn't live like I used to. "I had a moral dilemma in the feeding department," I explained shortly.

I expected him to scoff at me, but instead, he gave me a solemn look like he understood and respected me. "It is immoral to take without consent. It sullies the gift of blood. I am pleased an outsider also understands this. But you are old. The young have never been without as we have." He gave me that smile. The smile that spoke of years and cultures long past. It was a sweet secret the oldest of our kind shared. He led me to the hospital entrance and held the door open for me.

A limousine sat in the parking lot right in front of the entrance. Several humans stood around it, guarding its occupant. Wait. Were they humans? They didn't smell quite like humans. Kind of like how Knight didn't smell quite like Lycan. No, fuck. *Stop thinking about him.*

One of the not-humans opened the limo door, and their master stepped out of the vehicle as soon as we were close. He was tall with long white-blonde hair, and wore an expensive suit that probably cost as much as the limo. He looked young, about sixteen, but I could sense his age was older than Othello, though not by much. This Born was the leader of this town.

"So," he said when we were in front of him. "You're the

one who broke into the hospital." He was well informed, considering it had only been five minutes, ten at the latest, since Ahmed had found me. "The nurses were very concerned for you as you were so close to a frenzy."

"You spoke with them?" I asked him.

He looked me over like he was studying a work of art. I felt naked under his gaze. That was awkward considering he looked like he had barely left puberty. "We don't often get visitors, much less one of our kind."

I pulled my jacket closed, as if it would erase his eyes on me. "I didn't plan on running into a den of vampires. Your territory wasn't marked, I didn't smell it. I apologize."

"My name is James," he said as if I hadn't spoken. I had a slight feeling that he wasn't listening to anything I said, but I introduced myself anyway. He didn't react, again, and said to Ahmed, "Give her a room at the inn." He looked back at me, his eyes looking me over again. "I'll check in on you soon. I have business to attend to." His strange guards got into the limousine after him, then it pulled smoothly out of the parking lot and was gone with barely a crunch on the pavement.

"He's, uh..." I searched for a word that was more flattering than 'a fucking oddball.' Thankfully, Ahmed had a sense of humor and was already chuckling at me.

"I know. Not many of us are as old as James is. I suppose it's just his age."

I had a feeling it was more than that, but I held my tongue. Ahmed forwent a car, so we walked down the streets of James' city. It felt good to stretch my legs. It also felt foreign, being exposed like this, but I tried to forget about the past few months and just enjoyed my surroundings.

Every tree downtown was decorated with Christmas lights, as well as the edges of some of the buildings. It wasn't December, the decor was just something the humans enjoyed, Ahmed explained. I supposed that much light made them feel safer around so many vampires. Every street we walked through, our kind was intermixed with the humans. When we stopped at a park, Born were eating ice cream with humans, walking dogs with humans, some were even playing games with humans. I could easily see myself and Knight sitting on the grass together, laughing.

"You find it odd," Ahmed said after I'd been staring silently at the crowd in front of me. I nodded, no words coming to me. "We live in harmony here. There is no need to hide from them. They give us what we need –blood– and we protect them. There is only one rule. We do not turn them. Under any circumstance."

Then I realized that every vampire I'd seen was Born. None of the turned were among the masses. "Why?" I asked him. "Why don't you turn them?"

"Humans don't understand what it means to be a vampire. They think it means strength, power, and to be above humans. Better than humans. We are not better than anyone. Not humans. Not the Lycans. We are equals. We just... don't break as easily."

I chuckled at him. "A philosophy I'm used to living by."

The only thing I didn't see was Born and human couples, which was comforting, and made the oddness of the city slightly less odd. "The turned also don't listen. They're almost impossible to teach."

"Born have the ability to change and adapt. Humans are frozen in time when they drink our blood," he said back. It wasn't that I disagreed with him. I just always had the hope that it wasn't true. Deep down, I knew it was. "Here we are, the hotel."

We'd reached the end of a city block and stood in front of what was once a firehouse. It was now a small inn with two large wooden doors where the garage door used to be. Ahmed knocked once on the left door before it swung open revealing the proprietor, a plus-sized human woman with a kind smile and pink-tipped braids. I almost envied her curves since I was a beanpole, but I'd never felt inadequate in any area of my life. Well. Almost never. As I said, my breasts were tiny. She smiled at Ahmed and shifted her eyes to me. Her eyes scanned me and I felt something coming from her, a power that was rare among humans.

"You're a seer," I observed.

She laughed, making her jewelry jingle around. "That's an outdated word, but I'll take it. And yes. I am." Ahmed shifted his feet a few times before nodding his head to the human and walking back in the direction we came from. The female watched him go, her eyes turning to slits and a smile creeping on her face. When Ahmed turned a corner and disappeared from sight, she looked back at me. "Doesn't like humans, that one. Likes his nurses well enough, but he feeds from them. Ironic that we humans trust our health to a vampire that doesn't like us." She stopped talking and stood in the doorway for a minute. "Coming in?"

"I have to be invited."

She raised her eyebrows at me. "Damn, really? I've never heard that."

"No, not really. I'm just messing with you." I flashed my fangs at her in a smile and walked past the doorway into the hotel lobby. I caught her staring at me in a mirror, half unamused, half trying not to laugh. The lobby was clean and organized, if a little on the hippie side with the décor. Artwork covered the walls. Birds, clouds, trees, fire, and more, all beautifully painted. The human stood nearby while I surveyed the room, then gave me a look when I turned back to her that led me to believe these were her paintings. "They're lovely," I said with a smile. I wasn't lying, her work was really something. I'd never studied art seriously, but you pick up on a few things after decades of art enthusiasts peppering the walls of your house with paintings.

She relaxed a little. "Thanks. Means a lot coming from a vampire. An old one, I mean. I bet you knew all the old masters. Rembrandt, Monet, Van Gogh," she said with a sigh, pronouncing Van Gogh's name wrong. She'd also known I was old without asking.

"It's pronounced Goff," I corrected.

She pointed a finger at me. "Ha! So, you knew him? Was that ear cut off for you?"

"He was a chubby chaser, so, no."

She laughed loudly, slapping her leg a few times, and reached up to wipe her eyes when she'd calmed down. "Van Goff, a chubby chaser. Fuck, I like you." She sniffed and chuckled softly. "I'm Sara, the town weirdo."

I smiled at her. "A town is only as weird as the town weirdo."

She ran her hands down her sides. "I'm also lusciously curved. I can tell you noticed. Don't fib." I tried to come up with an excuse, but she waved her hand at me and giggled. "I'm just teasing. Curves are normal. You're a skinny thing, if you don't mind my saying. I've never seen anyone as skinny as you are. Do you eat enough?" I looked down and saw how loose my peasant blouse had become. When I'd bought it, it had fit me perfectly. I did look a little malnourished. "Stop, stop," she said suddenly, grabbing my wrists. "No need to be upset. You've always been skinny, right? We just need to fatten you up. I'll have a human here pronto that you can drink from."

"Thank you, but I'm full." I also had a stomachache, oddly enough. Did my breath smell? Not that it mattered.

"Alright, alright. If you say so." Sara tugged on one of her short pink-tipped braids while she maneuvered behind her large hotel type desk and fiddled with something underneath it. When she straightened up, she produced two large white towels. "These are unbelievably fluffy, you could sleep on them." She handed them to me and walked over to the stair-case. "Right this way." I followed her up, her hips moving from side to side in front of me. She turned to the left when we reached the landing and inserted a brass skeleton key into a door marked '1'. I was the only guest here, it seemed. She pushed the door open and held the key out to me. "A human will be in the lobby when you wake up, and I'll have food ready after you've fed. I'm thinking curry. You like spicy?"

"Curry for breakfast?"

"So that's a no. Okay. French toast waffles it is." She wiggled her fingers at me and went back down the stairs.

I sat down on the bed and let the towels fall to the floor. Could this town be my safe haven? If I gained James' favors, maybe he'd hide me from Arthur. Except Knight would never come here. I'd never see him again. Sniffing, I picked the towels back up. That would just be the price of my safety.

13

UNWANTED EVENTS

*D*espite the ridiculously comfortable bed, I didn't sleep well that night. My dreams were a mix of can-can dancers in Paris and Knight's passionate kisses. When I woke up, I half expected to find someone in bed with me, but my Bohemian-esque room was empty. Sara was very committed to the design of the room, down to very minute details, and I could tell she'd gotten the help of a vampire to make it historically accurate. The small bathroom attached to my room had a Steampunk theme, including a huge copper-colored claw foot bathtub. I managed to figure out the mechanics (and I mean mechanics literally) so I could take a bath. My skin was pale white again, but since I was in a town filled with my kind, I didn't need any tanning lotion.

After I cleaned up, I went downstairs and found a human male waiting for me on a red velvet couch. He introduced himself, Robert, and promptly left after I'd fed from him. As soon as he was gone, Sara waltzed in carrying a bowl of batter. Her hair was up in a scarf and she was wearing a loosely tied cocktail apron over a pajama top and pants with Tweety bird on them.

"Hey there, gorgeous! Ready for waffles?" I stood up and followed her to the tiny kitchen she'd come out of. There was a small table with two chairs in a 1950's style kitchen, complete with an avocado colored fridge. I sat down and Sara plunked a plate in front of me with three French toast waffles on it.

"This might be too much foo-"

"Nope. No arguments, missy. You'll eat it all and like it. Gotta fatten you up again. Can't have you sickly." Why did it matter to her if I stayed sickly? She finished cooking and sat down after removing her apron. Her pajama top rode up slightly, revealing stretch marks, the kind of stretch marks caused by being pregnant. She caught me staring so I looked back at my plate and started eating. "Nathan."

"What?"

"That's my son's name. But he goes by his middle name now."

"I didn't realize you're a mom." I hadn't seen toys around the hotel, nor heard anything during the night like a crying baby or a child asking for a glass of water.

"He's twenty," she said, like it wasn't weird.

I choked on my bite of French toast waffle. "You have a twenty-year-old son? You're so..."

"Young? Yeah. I was fifteen when I had him. His father was...dashing. He was an amazing lover, I will say." She smiled, a hazed look on her face. She cleared her throat and picked at her waffle. "Nathan works for his father."

I pointed to the vacant spaces around the table. "Only two chairs?"

"No one ever comes here, except for two people," she said quietly. "And they never come at the same time."

I wondered why James had told Ahmed to bring me to an inn that never had customers. "Well. You have someone here now," I said brightly. She smiled back at me.

The day went quietly and as slow as Christmas. I laid on the carpet in her living room, staring at the popcorn ceiling and trying to not think about a certain someone. We were eating a late lunch in the kitchen (eggs and kimchi) when there was a knock at the door. Sara, not looking the least bit surprised, left the kitchen and came back with an envelope and a large white gift box. She slid the box onto the table by my plate, handed me the envelope, and sat back down to finish her kimchi, a blank look on her face. I picked up the envelope and stole a glance at her but she was staring off into space, so I slid the seal open.

James was requesting my presence for dinner at his house tonight.

The box revealed a dress that designers dream about and

rich women drool over. Light brown satin with black lace on the bodice and edges, and an angled overskirt that went from knee to floor. Sara did a double take when she saw it and almost dropped her drink. Beside the dress was a small matching clutch, and shoes that made me want to cry. Designer clothes. I've missed you, my darlings. For one night at least, I could put aside my Bohemian hippie clothes and dress like I used to.

Sara got up, quickly washed our dishes, and disappeared.

I went upstairs and bathed again, then I put on makeup, did my hair, and then redid my hair a few more times before I was satisfied. By the time I was dressed and ready, I could hear a limo pull up outside. I went downstairs, sighing with happiness at the feel of heels, not to mention how much I loved this dress. Sara wasn't there to send me off.

One of the strange human bodyguards was standing by the limo door, waiting for me to get in. It smelled like pink champagne. When we reached James's home, correction: mansion, he wasn't there to greet me. I was led inside by my escort and guided to a sitting room. James sat in a large armchair with a small antique dining table set for two in front of him. A dainty boudoir chair was on the other side of the table, and it was almost too small even for my small ass. He smiled when he saw me in the doorway.

"Elisabeth, please come in," he said, gesturing to the chair across from him. How did he know my full name? I sat, feeling slightly uncomfortable at being given such a small chair. A display of power, most likely. "How are you liking the inn?" he asked, giving no indication he thought it was a bad establishment.

"It's good," I answered. "Sara is very kind. And she can really decorate."

James smiled, for the first time showing warmth. "Most people find her odd. I'm glad you do not." As if summoned silently, several humans came in bringing the first course: cucumber soup. "I wasn't sure which eras you preferred as far as cuisine is concerned, so I just went with some traditional favorites."

We ate, sometimes talking and appreciating shared experiences from the past, but mostly just enjoying the food. The main course was roast peacock, and the platter was decorated with several feathers, as well as the bird's head. I wrinkled my nose at it and James had it taken away with a snap of his fingers. Dessert came, an exotic chocolate dish, and he relaxed in his chair after finishing his.

"That was delightful," he said with a relaxed smile on his face. "Do you need to drink?" I shook my head. "I may after you leave. I usually do after I partake of food." He stood and walked over to examine a painting near my chair.

My brain didn't quite process that. "You drink more than once a day?"

He brushed his hand over his sleeves, even though they were spotless. "I drink as often as I feel like it."

"That causes instability." I'd lived long enough to know that. It would explain James's odd behavior. He was close to me now and held out a hand for me to take.

"It also causes powers. This you know."

I shifted my legs under the table. "I'm well aware."

"I can read minds. I can bend humans to my will. I can control our kind." He gave me a pointed look. "Including you."

"Well," I said quickly, tossing my cloth napkin onto the table. "This was a lovely meal, and I thank you for–" James interrupted me, uttering a single word.

"Stand."

My legs suddenly clenched, and the only thing I wanted to do was stand up.

I didn't.

His lips pursed at me and his eyes focused sternly on my face. "I said, stand." My muscles began to burn like I'd been sitting for days. I craved the sweet release standing would give me.

I still didn't.

This time James squinted, studying me, and a slow grin spread onto his face. "I should've known, given your age. There's only one way to make you submit." No. He couldn't mean... He pulled me by my hand to his embrace, and I felt revulsion having him so close to me. I fought, but he was stronger, and he held me against him forcefully.

Then he bit me.

14

FANGED

J rubbed my neck in the limo on the way back to
Sara's inn.

Once he'd bitten me, he kissed me for several minutes,
and man was it gross. Then he stroked my neck and told me
to go back to the hotel. He wasn't interested in hurting me,
which was nice. He just wanted to control me.

Sara was lounging on a fainting couch in the lobby when
I arrived, chewing on pieces of melon and reading a Japanese
newspaper upside down. She glanced up at me briefly and
went back to the paper. I could feel her disapproval, but of
what I had no idea. Then suddenly, she looked back at me
with a horrified expression and jumped up, tossing the paper
away.

"He bit you," she stated, her face shocked. I reached a
hand up to cover my neck. "He forced his will on you." She

put a hand on mine and gave me a comforting look, like James had raped me, instead of just biting me. Now that I thought about it, I wasn't sure how those two options differed.

Then the air changed. We both tensed, though I didn't know if Sara felt what I was feeling. It wasn't a smell, more like my ears had randomly tuned into something happening outside.

"He's here," she whispered.

I turned around and went back to the front door. Sara joined me, pulling on some shoes that looked like they'd come from Aladdin's closet. I expected to see James standing there, ready for round two of whatever he thought our evening had been, but that wasn't what greeted me.

Knight was further down the road, kneeling in the street, a dozen vampires and human bodyguards either holding him down or pointing a weapon at him. James stood at the head of the group, looking down at Knight, about to pass judgment for a Lycan trespassing within his unmarked borders.

Even though the last time I'd seen Knight had ended in literal blood and tears, I felt elation and relief at the sight of him. I'd given up hope that I'd ever see him again. And despite the oddness of our relationship, and my uncertainty about his intentions towards me romantically, I found I didn't want him to leave again.

"Wait!" I shouted. James's head turned to see Sara and I coming towards him. Two vampires had a rough grip on Knight's hair, but he fought his captors to find my face.

143

"Hey, Lisa," he said with a toss of his chin and a smile.

"Lisa?" I asked, dumbfounded. Did he forget my name? Was he playing dumb? Well. He didn't really have to play.

He grinned and my heart skipped a beat. "Trying to find you a nickname. Not working?"

The look I gave him was utter disbelief at his choice of conversation, given the circumstances. He shrugged and grinned playfully.

James hissed loudly so we'd stop talking. I felt the command, even if he hadn't spoken it. "You know this *mutt*, Elisabeth?" Knight's mouth wrinkled when my name was said as if he disapproved more of James using my full name than being called a mutt.

"Yes. He protected me before I came here. He's my–" I checked Knight's face before I finished my sentence, knowing I'd pay for it later. "–bodyguard." James started to chuckle ironically, and Knight scrunched his mouth up even more with annoyed disapproval.

"I can see that you're serious," James said after he'd finished laughing. "You had your reasons for hiring a mongrel to watch over you, I suppose." Mongrel? That was much worse than dog. Even I was offended. "What shall you do with him?"

That surprised me. "The fuck?"

"He bears your scent. You've bitten him. You decide what his fate is. Shall we kill him?" He waited for me to speak. To choose.

I glanced back at Knight, still kneeling on the asphalt and

being restrained by so many other bodies, much more than a normal man would require. "Let him go." I caught a slight nod from James out of the corner of my eye before Knight was released. He stood and brushed off his faded blue jeans.

"Thanks, Lis," he said, the grin back on his face.

James straightened and flicked a hand for everyone to give Knight more space. "I expect you gone from my city before sunrise," he commanded the Lycan.

"No, he's not leaving," I said, and instantly regretted it.

James's body turned and seemed to tower over me. "Excuse me?"

I swallowed, fear trickling up my skin, and Knight gave me a perplexed look. It took all my power not to stutter. "I want him to stay."

"Are you defying me?" James asked sternly.

I whimpered. It felt as if weights were crushing me and I struggled to breathe. I couldn't defy my master. My panicked eyes went back to Knight. Although he didn't know what was going on, he at least wasn't mad at me for being a weakling. Wait. I wasn't defying James.

"You..." I swallowed. "You said I decide his fate. I want him to stay here." I waited to feel pain, weakness, the crushing weights again, but I didn't.

James humphed at me, a smile coming to his lips. "Clever. Very well. You win this time." He raised two fingers and made a circle in the air, which meant the show was over. The humans and vampires dispersed. With a smile still on his face, he took my arm and squeezed it so hard his nails pierced my thick vampire skin before he forced me to kiss him.

Ewwwwwww.

"Be glad I enjoy your companionship, Lisbeth." And with that, he was gone, along with his bodyguards.

Knight ran his hands through his mussed hair. "Nice company you're keeping, Lis." My emotions swirled so badly, I didn't how to react. Sara broke the silence, stepping forward and offering her hand to him.

"I'm Sara. Resident weirdo."

He took her hand and pumped it a few times. "Nice to know you're owning it." She shrugged playfully and flipped some of her pink-tipped hair back. Was she flirting?

I interrupted... whatever they were up to. "What are you doing here?" I asked Knight sternly.

"Aaaand moment over. I'll be in the lobby." Sara about faced with a fancy twirl and half ran back to the hotel.

Knight watched her leave (was he checking her out?), then he turned back to me. His face softened slightly. "Are you his now?"

"That's not what I fucking asked you."

"Fine. I was worried about you."

My first reaction was accusatory. Why had he left? Why had he suddenly come back? But I was too relieved to see him and too tired to argue. "The reason being?"

"I caught your scent at the gas station outside of town, and then I smelled other vampires. I figured you'd been captured."

In the midst of everything that had happened in the past hour, I'd scarcely thought of Arthur. But that didn't matter much now since I was bound to the small city and couldn't leave without James's permission. I'd have to take my chances with the Hunters, as disconcerting as that was. I had bigger problems at the moment.

"Thank you for the concern," I told Knight. "I haven't been found yet, so I'm safe."

He looked at the corner of the street, the one James had disappeared behind. "Forgive me if I don't believe you."

15

THE INSANITY PERSISTS

*O*nce we were secure in my hotel room, Knight shut and locked the door before turning to me with a very determined look on his face.

"You're going to tell me everything that happened here," he said firmly, his arms crossed over his broad chest.

"I don't think I owe you anything," I countered, arms over my chest as well. I hadn't been mad before that moment, but now I was so upset with him for abandoning me, it was overriding my happiness that he was standing in front of me.

His eyes fell to my neck and his expression turned dark. "Did he bite you?"

My hand automatically went up to cover it. "Yes."

"Fucking bastard," he ground out. He moved towards me, hands out, probably to look at the wound, but I recoiled away from him.

148

"Please don't touch me," I whimpered. "I feel extremely violated right now, I can't deal with physical touch." Tears came down my cheeks and I sniffed with a sigh. "I'm sorry."

His brown eyes looked as sad as I'd ever seen them. "Don't be. I won't touch you." I nodded, wiping my cheeks. He grabbed a blanket from the bed and went to sleep on the floor without another word.

***

I slept fitfully, my dreams running over and over what it felt like to have my free will taken from me so easily. It was as foreign to me as being human. I'd never experienced anything like it before, and that was saying something. When I woke up the next morning, my pillow was soaked with sweat. Knight's pallet had been neatly folded up and he wasn't in the room. I took a bath, got dressed, and went downstairs.

When I walked into the kitchen, Knight and Sara were eating breakfast. They both had a similar look of cautious pity when they saw me. I sat down in the chair Sara had brought into the room for me, a wicker armchair that didn't match the 1950's kitchen theme. She'd already loaded a plate for me with pancakes that smelled like chocolate chips and cannoli. I brought a fork towards the stack and Sara quickly added a mess of whipped cream on top.

"Gotta keep your strength up. You didn't sleep well last night," Sara said cheerfully. She added one more extra-large squirt of foam for good measure before setting the can down. "Oh! I almost forgot. I didn't get you someone to drink from. Silly me. Oh, and Knight, please don't break more of my dishes." She waltzed out without another word.

Knight looked down at his plate, still covered in a half-eaten stack of chocolate chip and cannoli pancakes. "I haven't broken her dishes," he said in confusion.

"She's always saying things like that, don't worry. She's a seer," I told him. I took a bite of my own breakfast and suddenly didn't want to talk anymore. It was that good. I wanted to break down and cry at the deliciousness.

"Like, oooo you will meet a mysterious stranger?" he asked, clearly skeptical.

"Like seeing the future is any weirder than having a freaky moon relationship?"

He twirled his fork around mockingly. "Meh, meh, meh, I drink blood."

That's how the food fight started.

We flung pieces of pancake at each other and both grabbed whipped cream to attack with. I clobbered him with a giant spray of cream, and he grabbed me to him to put his supply in my hair.

"No!" I screamed. "Not my hair, you cuntwaffle!" He laughed and his smile fell as he reached up to push my hair back. I realized I was in his arms, and I pulled away. "Sorry."

Looking away, he sighed and flicked me with cream. "Stop apologizing to me."

When Sara came back into the room, Knight, the kitchen, and I were covered in pancakes and canned whipped cream.

"I'd be furious at you two, but I'm more furious that you won't be able to help me clean this up. Plate." Knight was turning to see her and his foot slipped on the floor. His hand reached for the table to stop his fall and he knocked his plate off the corner. It crashed onto the floor. "Like I said, please don't break more of my dishes. I like those. They're vintage."

"Sorry," he apologized. "We'll help clean up."

She sighed like she was tired of people not listening to her. "I said you two won't be able to help me clean. Did you not hear?" She turned to me. "I couldn't get you someone to drink from. This was at the door." She handed me a letter and shooed us out of the kitchen.

"What's that?" Knight asked, his finger scraping a big glob of whipped cream off his arm that he popped into his mouth. The envelope was sealed with red wax and the impression of a ring. I didn't recognize the symbol, but I didn't have to guess who had sent it.

I've sent a car for you. You may drink at my home every morning.'

Easily a message he could've said over the phone or something. Knight took the paper and read it. He didn't say anything so I explained what it meant.

"He wants to control my feeding."

Knight nodded and handed the paper back. "I figured as much." He focused on something near my arm, and I was about to ask what it was until he reached a finger out to scoop up another glob of cream that sat on my elbow.

"Eww!" I ran back up the stairs so he couldn't eat any left-over breakfast on me.

"I'm hungry! You interrupted a perfectly good stack of pancakes, COME BACK HERE!"

We cleaned up and went outside. The stretch limo James had sent was still sitting there waiting at the end of the block. More of his not-human guards were there. Knight wrinkled his nose at them, their odd smell disagreeing with his brain.

"What are they?" I shrugged. I was just as clueless. "They were fucking strong last night. Way too strong to be human." We'd reached the limo, and the closest not-human came up to stand in our way. I recognized him from the scuffle the previous night and from when I'd first met James. He had blonde hair and his features were similar to James', not to mention their eyes were the same color. His son?

"He is not allowed to join you," the not-human said, inclining his head at Knight. I didn't want Knight to leave me since I was feeling incredibly vulnerable in this town, but it was safer to not piss James off.

"Fine," I told him. I gave Knight a wave and walked over to step inside the car. The guards got in behind me and the limo took off. Inside the limo, there was a small mini-fridge and a bowl of wrapped chocolate mints. I took one and chewed it while we drove to James's house.

I looked the not-human up and down. "What's your name," I asked around the chocolate mint.

He glanced over at me and gave me a look like I could use a brush-up on manners. "Drake."

"You have the same eyes as James," I told him. I was so nervous, I couldn't stop myself from talking.

"He's my father," Drake said simply. Called it!

"But you're..." I started. He waited for me to finish my sentence, but I wasn't sure what I was going to say. You're human but not human? Thankfully, he was content to ignore me so I didn't have to continue the conversation.

It wasn't a long trip to James' mansion, small town and all, and soon the limo was going up a small incline before it stopped. The guards got out, opened the door for me, and helped me step out. James' mansion looked the same, but a little less welcoming. It was in the early American style, a colonial mansion. The type people used to have parties and balls at before the American Revolution. I'd been too distracted to really notice it before. He might have been a psycho overlord, but he had a nice house.

The inside was decorated with vintage furniture, no doubt all original from when the house was first built. You'd be surprised how long a chair can last when it's not seeing daily use. The walls had dozens of paintings and photographs. While only some of the paintings were of James, all the photographs were of him, captured at various points in time, and harkening all the way back to the first cameras.

Then Drake led me to a sitting room. James was sprawled on a divan, two female humans on either side of him. One had bite marks above her collarbone that trickled blood he hadn't bothered to clean up. That was considered extremely fucking disrespectful, but I wasn't about to call him on it.

His face brightened when he saw me. "Lisbeth! Come. Have a drink with me. I saved you one." He pushed at the other female's side until she stood up and came halfway to me. He'd ordered to me to drink, but it hadn't been entirely direct. I still felt the compulsion behind it as I walked up to the female without hesitation. She was taller than me so I lifted her arm and sunk my fangs into it, making sure to miss the artery that ran to her elbow. I didn't want her to bleed out. Her blood tasted bitter, and I knew I'd get a stomach ache from it. I drank as much as I needed before pulling away, making sure to lick her skin around my bite to clean off the residual blood. I had to resist the urge to gag over the foul taste of her. I was sure she wouldn't appreciate being told she tasted bad.

James was watching me with a steady gaze, one of his hands gently stroking the hair of the female he'd fed from. "Are you satisfied?" I nodded. "Good. Ladies, shoo." He waved his hand at them and they left together. "Have you eaten?" I nodded again. "Not feeling chatty this morning? Never mind. I can talk for the both of us."

Oh fuck me.

He got up smoothly and walked over to me. One hand reached up to swipe my hair off my shoulder, and he leaned in to place a gentle kiss on his bite mark.

"I hated doing that," he said mournfully, and I wanted to recoil from his fingers traipsing over my skin. "If you'd been weaker, I wouldn't have needed to. But you're old." He kissed higher on my neck. "I'm glad to see you don't protest to being called old. Most of the younger vampires don't understand. It's not an insult to us. To humans, it means you're closer to death. To us, it means you've been alive longer." His lips went to my ear and I almost let out a noise of displeasure. "Have you ever wondered why there are so few older Born?"

"Sometimes."

He stepped away from me and picked up a drink from the coffee table, then he swirled the amber liquid in the glass. "I've often thought about it. No one really knows for sure why. There are so many rumors surrounding the topic that one can hardly discern any actual facts. Since you're barely younger than me, I'd be interested to know your thoughts on the matter." He waited for me to speak, staring me down while he took a long sip from his glass.

I couldn't lie, I'd often wondered about this topic. Why me, a 400-year-old vampire, was considered one of the oldest when vampires had been around for many millennia, but I didn't exactly feel like having a heart to heart with James.

I gave him a simple answer. "There are certain topics my Order prefers not to discuss. That's one of them."

"Oh, fuck that. I asked what you think, not what your Order thinks. That's why I stay away from the Orders. They're all rules and regulations. Not at all to my taste. Stuffy pricks." *Stuffy.* That did explain why he was here, ruling over his own little world, and why I'd never heard of him.

"I'm sure they wouldn't approve of your feeding schedule," I said before I could stop myself.

He studied me and then smiled slowly as if he'd figured me out. "You were a rule enforcer, weren't you?" I stayed silent. "A rule enforcer on the run for breaking the rules. How's that irony for you? Stop being so uptight. I despise uptight people."

Did he seriously bring me here just to talk about how stuffy I am? And he'd just ordered me to stop being uptight too. Might as well order me to stop being sarcastic.

I cleared my throat casually, trying to hold in the pain I felt as his order seeped in. "Did you need anything else?"

"Hmm, dinner tonight. Leave." And with that, he dismissed me. And I gladly left.

16

THE PARTY OF PAIN

*J*ames sent over another outfit for me to wear when the limo arrived and this one was a deep purple cocktail dress with a low back. I put it on and left in the limo.

'Dinner with James' was apparently also 'Party with James.' His colonial mansion was littered with the rich and fabulous from this tiny town. Mostly Born, some humans. I exited the limo and went to the front door. Drake was there to wave me in, ignoring me as much as possible. Whatever he was, he did not like me, a fact I was fine with.

Inside the mansion, it took me a few minutes to find James. He was in the thick of it, in the parlor I'd been in that morning, surrounded by humans and Born, dominating all the attention with whatever he was telling them. He spotted me and brightened, then he walked to me, motioning me closer.

"Lisbeth, how good to see you," he said, leaning in to kiss my lips. Unable to help it, I recoiled at the unwanted contact, but he held me firmly. "Don't recoil from me," he whispered in my ear. My body crunched inward at his order like he'd squeezed my ribcage, and I tried not to lean against him as I swayed with pain. He stepped away, put a hand on my bare back in an unwanted caress, and pushed me towards his friends. "Gentlemen, meet Lisbeth. My latest conquest."

His conquest. That put a lot of things into perspective.

"We have been so excited to meet you," one of them said, a human female decked to the teeth in pearls.

"A vampire almost as old as our master, you are a precious gem," another said, this one a male vampire wearing a very expensive suit. James tightened his hold around me as if he was jealous of anyone saying how awesome I was. My hip bone felt slightly crushed under his hand. I knew I'd have a bruise there later.

"James," someone purred in a heavy accent. A female vampire came up to us and offered James her hand, which he gently kissed. She glanced at me, gave me a once-over, and smiled at me in a way that meant she wanted to rip my hair out. "So, you're her. The vampire that was so strong, James had to bite you." She clearly ranked being bitten by James with winning the lottery. And I was almost positive her accent was fake. "He's never had to bite one of us before. Carrying his mark means being under his absolute control.

Having to obey his every whim. If only one of us could be so lucky," she said, with a cute little seductive laugh at the end.

I wisely held my tongue, even though she was waiting for me to say something. I didn't think James would appreciate me telling his guest to go fuck herself.

"Don't be so jealous, Miranda," James said playfully. "I can still control you."

She gave him a look that wasn't very appropriate for a room full of people. "Yes, but I can say no. She cannot." She looked back over at me. "Your lady looks like she doesn't want to be here. Maybe she should go home and leave you with us." Oh, yes, please.

James laughed. "Don't be ridiculous, Miranda. Why don't you go get another drink?" She left in an unsatisfied huff. James leaned into me and said harshly, "Cheer up. Stop looking like you don't want to be here." I instantly smiled and looked like I was having the time of my life.

And that's how it went for hours.

Order after order. Don't leave my side. Kiss me like you mean it. Stop fidgeting. Dance with me. Don't dance with anyone else. Only look happy when you're with me. Stop looking unhappy. Try the veal.

He spouted out orders so often, he didn't know which he'd already said to me, or which contradicted each other. I had a feeling he didn't even realize he was causing me pain. With every order, my body hurt more and more. I didn't have to think about obeying, I naturally did that, but my body was suffering being under his control. It fought underneath at the sheer wrongness of it all, and I was racked with pain in every part of my body.

When James finally said I could leave, after everyone else had gone, the only thing keeping me up was his order to stop looking like I was about to fall over. He put me inside one of his limos, giving me a slow kiss on the lips, and sent me on my way.

The further I got from him, the more pain I felt. Wave after wave of agony. Every sound was too loud, every light was too bright. If I had to deal with this for the rest of my life, I would go insane. Drake sat there the entire time, either not noticing how much I was hurting, or not caring.

When the limo pulled up to Sara's hotel, Drake helped me out, and I stood on unsteady limbs that barely supported my weight. I walked slowly to the front door and put my hand on the handle. It opened before I could try to pull on it.

Sara stood in the doorway, her face the most serious I'd seen in our short friendship. I stumbled over the threshold and didn't put a hand up fast enough to stop myself from bonking my nose on the doorway.

"That vile man," Sara whispered. Even her soft voice pounded in my head, and I whimpered, putting a hand to my face to shield my eyes from the lights. I noticed Knight coming into the lobby from the kitchen, but I couldn't bear to look at him. I felt so much shame. And pain. Lots of pain. The light bothering me was suddenly gone, and a hand reached out to stroke my hair.

Without a word, Knight took my hand and led me up to

my room. He walked over to shut the curtains to block out the moonlight before coming back to stand in front of me. The darkness didn't bother our superior eyesight. I could still see him as well as if the light was on.

Someone knocked so lightly on the door I almost didn't hear it. Sara peeped her head in and placed a bottle on the floor before closing the door again. Knight bent to pick it up and studied the label. He showed it to me. Sky Vodka.

Vampires can't really get drunk, but we could get a nice buzz with a good percentage in our system. I grabbed the bottle and swigged half of it before Knight grabbed it back to chug the rest.

I wiped my mouth and looked up at him. "I don't want to talk about it," I said quietly. My own voice made my temple throb.

Knight didn't respond. He set the empty bottle down on the floor and approached me slowly, judging my response to his proximity. When he was so close I could feel his breath on my hair, I put my arms around him and I cried harder than I'd ever cried before.

17

HE'S PASSABLE

*M*y head was still throbbing when I woke up, but everything else felt better. I sat up and crawled to the edge of the bed. Knight was lying on the floor, one arm behind his head, the other holding his phone that he was playing a game on. He looked up at me and put his phone away.

"Morning," he said quietly, a sleepy smile on his face. Beautiful. He was so beautiful.

I wanted to slide off the bed and just fall onto the floor next to him, probably cry again, but I didn't. Instead, I just felt more shame.

"I'm sorry," I said, staring at the floor beside him. "I'm sorry if I made you uncomfortable last night."

"That's what the vodka was for," he joked. "I was more worried about you." I didn't respond, so he added, "You smelled like tacos." Tacos? How could I have smelled like tacos?

"There weren't tacos at the party."

"Okay, maybe I was the one that smelled like tacos. Either way, I really want tacos now." He put two fingers to his temple and pretended to concentrate.

"What are you doing?"

"I'm sending Sara a psychic vibe so she'll make me tacos." He narrowed his eyes and grunted with effort. "Damn," he said as he relaxed. "It was worth a try." He saw me looking at him so he met my eyes. "Don't worry about me, Lis. I'm here for you when you need me. That's what friends are for."

Was he my friend? I hated to put a label on what we were. Calling him my friend wasn't bad though, just unexpected. Whatever my feelings for him were, he thought of me as a bloodsucker.

"We're friends?" I asked tentatively.

He looked at me like I'd just said I had an imaginary friend. "Of course we're friends, dumb-dumb. I didn't come here for someone I hate."

And yet, despite everything, it was the first time he'd ever said he felt something higher than repulsion for me. He knew it, by the look on his face, and he wouldn't meet my eyes again. Sara knocked on the door and I heard him whisper, "Tacos, tacos, tacos," like he was praying.

"Everyone decent?" she asked as she stepped into the room too quickly for anyone to say no. "I made croissants with custard filling."

I was speechless. "That's my favorite food," I said in complete shock. I mean, I knew she had powers, but she was good. Like, really good. Which I'd guessed, so I probably shouldn't have been so surprised.

She nodded happily at me with a secret grin. "I know. You need some armor this week. Nothing helps quite like your favorite food." She glanced down at Knight, who was waiting patiently for her to announce that she was also making tacos. She didn't.

Sara had made enough custard croissants to feed ten people. My plate alone could've fed Knight for two meals. She was well on her way to fattening me up, as if that was even possible.

I ate half of what she'd given me and fell into a food coma on the bed. When I woke up, Knight was sitting next to me, reading a book on Civil War history. He didn't look up when I stirred.

"Is that accurate?" I asked him. I sat up and stretched my arms.

He shrugged. "Kind of one-sided. Leaves out a lot." He put it down and leaned his head back against the back of the bed.

I tuned my ears into the rest of the house and found it empty. "Where's Sara?"

"Grocery shopping. She said she was going to need more

pickles." I giggled. She was a refreshing person. "Speaking of food, you're due at James's for blood." He said it matter-of-factly like I was going there to get my mail, then he gave me a thoughtful look. "In all this time, I've never asked. What do your kind think of mine?"

I held out my fingers to tick off a list. "Dirty. Gross. Hump everything. Something about fleas." He shoved me with a pillow. "Serious, we do actually think you're dirty like you don't shower or something. And you're gross because you procreate with humans. Eww," I emphasized. "Also, no self-control, and you get pissed at everything."

He conceded to that. "That applies to the Lycans. Not me. And I totally shower every day."

"I never said I thought those things, by the way," I added. "I thought you were... passable when we first met."

He chuckled, and I could see him remembering that day. "I was basically disgusted with you."

"How about now?" I asked cautiously, trying to be casual.

He thought about it, a half smile on his face, and I felt almost scared of what his answer would be. "50% less icky."

"That's so generous of you," I said with a sarcastic smile, oddly relieved. "You're 35% less passable."

"Awwww, so mean. I think I earned at least 42%. Can I call a friend?"

"Sorry, ballot is out."

He pelted me with a pillow until I said he was 38% less passable.

18
THE PROPOSAL

With James, it was the same thing every day. I went to his house in the morning and drank from whoever he chose for me. Every day, he kissed me. Just kisses, thankfully. And before he would let me leave, he would brush my hair back and admire his bite. It hadn't faded, no matter how many days passed.

At night, he threw various parties.

The orders he'd given me at that first party were all side comments, and they'd carried weight while I was near him. He knew that, so he was careful to make other orders direct commands that I couldn't disobey, no matter how far away he got.

Sometimes when I left his house in the morning, he'd order me to ignore everyone, or stay indoors, or not speak.

Sometimes he made me stay at his house all day and just sit there, not moving.

It was torture.

The worst days were when I wasn't allowed to see Knight. He made everything seem a little brighter, even if it wasn't.

About a week had passed when I was sent an invitation to the opera. James had been mentioning it for several days, but he hadn't set a date yet. There was a youth orchestra here, probably funded by him, and a group of actors that put on performances. James wanted an opera, so they were putting on an opera.

He sent a dress, as usual, and I started getting ready. Sara never helped me. Whenever she saw that I'd been sent clothes, she would disappear into a random room of the hotel until I returned, broken and sobbing. I cried a lot now. Knight was always there. Sometimes he let me hug him while I cried, but only when we'd both had some alcohol first. And he always made me laugh the next morning.

The dress from James was a masterpiece. Black lace, long flowing skirt, decorated with dozens of small black butterflies that danced up the dress to rest on one shoulder and flutter near the even smaller butterflies in my hair. This was a dress I would've chosen for myself, and I hated that I had to wear it to something I wasn't looking forward to.

When Knight saw me, he looked a little surprised at the way I looked. I'd spent extra time looking pretty. Not for James. For myself.

"You clean up good," Knight appraised, the expression on his face as calm as I'd ever seen him. That was it? I clean up good? I looked fucking hot, you twat! He helped me lift the bulk of my skirt into the car and I left the hotel with Drake at the wheel.

The opera hall was surprisingly very nice, looking incredibly authentic to the old 19th-century theatres, with decorative gold plating on everything, and plush red carpets. It looked almost exactly like certain rooms in the Order. Ah, nostalgia.

James saw me enter the lobby after Drake dropped me off, and he smiled widely at me. "Lisbeth, my dear." He came up and kissed me on the lips, deeply, like I was his lover. I didn't kick him in the dick. I was under orders. "You look amazing. Even a fool can see how gorgeous you look." Apparently, he thought I cleaned up good too. "You are going to love this opera. It's one of my favorites." I'd read the playbill on the ride over, not to mention I'd already seen this opera over thirty years ago, but I played along.

"I can't wait," I told him with a plastered on smile. He put a hand to my back and led me up to one of the opera boxes, all the while describing the plot of the opera, and spoiling more than a little of the ending. The theatre opened out before me as I stepped into the opera box. It was just as beautiful and breathtaking as the outside and lobby had been. I felt more nostalgia, but for memories that had nothing to do with the Order. It made me relax a little, just remembering happier times. I sat down in one of the two chairs and James sat next to me.

The orchestra was still warming up, so I had time to look around the theatre at the other occupants. There were more opera boxes, all full, but ours was not close to any of them. We had as much privacy as you can get in a dim theatre with vampires that can see in the dark.

"Lisbeth," James said over the orchestra tuning. "There's something I want to discuss with you." Any relaxation I'd gained was gone. My body tensed up instantly, and I waited with dread for him to keep talking. Would it be more commands, or would he finally order me to get rid of Knight?

Was he going to hurt me?

"I've greatly enjoyed our time together, as you know. I'm pleased that you're so cooperative." What the fuck. "So, I've decided something, but this isn't an order. This is something you are absolutely allowed to say no to." Brilliant. Please ask me if I want to leave.

"What is it?" I hesitantly asked him with a smile.

He took one of my hands, reverently, with a familiarity we didn't have, even with all his forced kisses. "I'd like you to become my mate."

Mother. Fucker.

He patted my hand, mistaking my shock/rage for excitement. "I know. It's breathtaking, catching my attention, but you have. You absolutely have."

He was absolutely fucking insane.

"And if I refuse?"

That made him pause, looking for all the world like that hadn't even crossed his mind. "Like I said, you are allowed to refuse. Should you decide you don't want to become my mate, I'll put you in some housing on the edge of town. The dog will have to go, but that won't be a problem, I'm sure. I may require you to have one of my children, however, that will be many years in the future."

"So," I spoke slowly. "If I refuse, I still have to stay here?"

He bellowed out a laugh like I was a child that had just said something cute. "Of course, you adorable creature. I'm not letting you leave. You're staying here forever." I took my hand back but he didn't notice, he was so caught up with his crazy thoughts. I'd escaped one prison only to be caught in another. And this one was worse. I'd put up with all of this on the mere hope that soon James would be done with me and say I could be on my way, but he wasn't going to, and that made my situation more dangerous than I'd thought it was.

19

SOMETHING GIVES

I didn't say much during the rest of the opera. James seemed happier, more relaxed, after getting that weight off his shoulders. Lucky him. When we were in the lobby during intermission, he decided to pretend as if this was the age of chaperones and stolen kisses. He stood close to me, but not too close, and every so often he'd hold my hand when he thought no one was looking, and let it go again if someone noticed. As intermission ended, I half expected him to bring a chaperone back into the box with us, but he didn't. He did, however, giggle, and say he felt wicked being alone in the dark with me.

I really wanted to facepalm myself hard enough to punch a hole in my face. Or just punch a hole in *his* face.

He was always weird. That wasn't new. But he was usually mature weird. This was putting him to bed with no dinner weird. And I was so sick of it, I wanted to jump off the balcony and be impaled on something sharp.

When the opera ended, he insisted on walking me home. He nodded his head to everyone who passed, his face never losing that giddy grin. When we finally rounded the corner to Sara's hotel, Drake was standing next to a limo waiting out front for James, and my feet had gone bloody from walking in the heels I was wearing.

James took me to the door and everything giddy wiped away, as if it had never happened. He looked completely serious, the way he normally did. "Thank you for the lovely evening, Lisbeth." He took my hand and kissed it. "I will expect your answer soon." I nodded and he turned around, walking stiff-backed to the limo as Drake opened the door for him. He got in and the limo drove away.

Fucking Christ.

I took off my heels and stepped into the hotel. The lobby was empty, no Sara to greet me as usual, and no Knight to help put me back together. I stumbled up to my room and sank down onto the bed, the poufy skirt of my dress all around me. I sat there for a long time, mulling over everything that had led me to this moment. I didn't want to cry about this. Crying meant I was stretched too thin. I felt more like I'd just been broken, and I was too destroyed to cry about it.

I'd never get away from here. Knight would leave me. Arthur would eventually find me, and I'd be executed. That threat seemed so far away, but it was there.

I'd been there for over an hour when Knight knocked on the door. He handed me a glass of water and sat down in a chair in front of me. I wanted to ask where he'd been this whole time, but he wasn't my servant. He could do whatever the fuck he wanted. Including leave, which he would when he found out I was stuck here forever. His ass would be gone with the snap of a finger.

"Sara," he said quietly, breaching the silence. "Sara said I couldn't come out until now. She was quite adamant. She even made tacos to bribe me." I smiled, but it faded quickly. "She also said he was going to do something that would, and I quote, 'Break the camel's back.' So, spill."

I took a sip of my water and stared at the perfect ice cubes. "He proposed."

"That's fucking gross."

"But he said I could say no."

"Not as gross."

"Saying no would mean relocating me to the edge of town, and having his child at some point."

"Okay, what the fuck."

"Also kicking you out."

"His loss."

"And..." I swallowed and set my glass down on the nightstand. "He said I can't leave. Ever." My cheeks were wet and a sob escaped from my lips. Knight was there in an instant, pulling me up and into his arms. "You can't go. I need you. I don't know why, but I need you. And I shouldn't need you."

"Because I'm a wolf?"

That was the thought that had run through my mind since the day we'd met, and when I searched through my heart, I found the answer had changed. "I don't care what you are."

"Good." He crashed his lips against mine, and everything felt right.

I broke from his lips and whispered, "You said I repulsed you."

He laughed and kissed me so passionately, I felt like I was going to burn up. "I lied."

I needed his lips like I needed air. More air. More Knight. I tugged on the edge of his shirt and he helped me pull it over his head, coming back to my lips in a fevered rush. Flames licked all over my body and he hadn't even touched me yet.

"Touch me," I pleaded with a gasp and tunneled my hands through his long black hair to bring his mouth in for more kisses. His fingers found my hips and he roughly pulled me flush against him.

That was *definitely* not a phone in his pocket.

I rocked my hips against him and he moaned in my mouth. The strapless opera dress slipped off with one tug from his hands, baring my breasts to his view. They were tiny by normal standards, but he stared at them like they were precious gems he'd been searching for his whole life. His head dipped and he captured one nipple in his teeth and I almost came apart at the seams. I had no plans to orgasm just from him biting my nipple, but shit, I was close.

He switched to the other nipple, making me moan and wiggle against him, and he held me still so he could slide his fingers into the waistband of my panties. They slowly moved down to the giant wet spot on my cotton briefs and he let go of my nipple long enough to whisper heatedly, *"Fuck."* I gently pulled on his hair to bring his lips to mine again, and we kissed deeply as his fingers found my hot spot. It was so sensitive, I gasped and bucked against his hand. Every stroke against my clit was like magic. I'd never felt this much desire for anyone, ever. Not in 400 years. His fingers played a dance over my nub and I was dying for release.

He whispered in my ear, "Come for me."

Shit. That was all I needed, and I was falling into the abyss. The only thing holding me together was his lips and body as my orgasm took over me. Gasping over and over, I writhed in ecstasy, and he kissed every inch of my neck while I came down. I couldn't breathe, I couldn't think.

Best. Orgasm. Ever.

He took his hand from my panties and held me close for another breathtaking kiss. My fingers moved down to his pants and I managed to slide my palm up the hardness I found there before he stopped me.

"No, we shouldn't do that," he cautioned, and kissed me again feverishly, making sure I knew he still wanted me. "If we become lovers, James will smell it. You know the scent of our kind changes when we have a lover. It's safer to wait until we're out of here." He kissed my forehead gently. "Lis." I looked up at him and stared into his deep brown eyes. "If there was ever a time to break free from him, now is the time to do it."

My eyes started stinging in defeat. "I don't know how. I barely knew this type of control existed, I have no idea how to get free."

"So you spent all your time walled up in that castle and you didn't bother to learn anything about how your own kind work?" he snapped in irritation, shutting his eyes and sighing to calm himself down. "Sorry, I'm sorry." His lips kissed me gently.

"It's forbidden," I said feebly once he'd let my lips go. It was the excuse I'd been saying for a long time, over a lot of different things.

"Being informed shouldn't be forbidden, Lis. You have to know how to combat what's not allowed instead of just ignoring it."

I kissed him this time and wrapped my arms around his neck. "Hunters know. Olivier would know."

He looked hopeful. Much more hopeful than I was. "Can you contact her?"

"I'm not sure," I said. "It'd be dangerous, for me at least. Maybe Sara could help."

We made a plan and got to work.

I slept with dreams of the French Revolution and woke up to Olivier sitting at the end of the bed wearing Hunter gear.

Knight was sleeping beside me and she was eyeing him like he'd gotten dirt on her shoes. I gasped and sat up, looking around for Arthur.

"He's not here," she said in a weary tone. "I'm alone. Which is good news for the dog. I think. I got your message." Sara had left a message with Renard, who then got in touch with Olivier and told her we needed to meet with her. "Lisbeth, you can't stay in this town. We're so close to catching you, and if you stay still, we'll find you. Arthur will take you back to the castle." To execute me, most likely. It pained me, but I had to tell her.

"I can't."

"What are you talking about? Did you not hear me?"

I pulled my shirt aside to show the bite. Her reaction was worse than Sara's. She brought her hands to her mouth in utter horror and then worried her fingers around the bite like a mother trying to make a skinned knee feel better. Worse still, she hugged me so tightly I could feel my chest creak. When she pulled back she had tears in her eyes, and she touched the bite again with a mournful look. Then she breathed deeply to shake it off and took my shoulders.

"You have to fight back."

"I don't know how. That's why we contacted you."

She shook me a little. "Focus. You can break free. But..."

I gave her a questioning look. "But what?"

"It means breaking some rules. But you're already on the run, so what the hell. Let's go crazy." She looked over at Knight's sleeping form on the bed, then back at me. "Are you drinking from him regularly? I can smell you on him." I shrugged one shoulder, non-committal, almost ashamed. She leaned forward to whisper in my ear, "Was it gross?" I playfully shoved her away and thought I heard a noise coming from Knight's pillow. "Okay, business talk. Whether you drink from the dog, eww, or from a human, you need to be drinking several times per day. Four at the least."

"Four? The side effects will be monstrous."

"I know the side effects. I've lived the side effects. It has to be done. Unless you feel like being captured by us, or staying here to be this James' lady friend until you die. Or both."

"Not really."

"Good girl." She glanced at Knight again and reached out with one heavily buckled boot to lightly kick his leg. "You. Get up. I know you're not sleeping." He rolled over and sat up, wide awake.

"She can drink from me," he affirmed, without any prompting. He locked eyes with me. That would mean helping me in a way he had only done once, and that time had been an emergency. At least we were kind-of lovers now. Right?

"I didn't ask," Olivier said back, even though she'd definitely not excluded his blood as a possibility a mere moment ago.

His eyes narrowed at her. "And I wasn't offering. I'm telling."

Olivier's nails started to grow from where they sat on her

shorts, scratching her dark brown legs slightly. With a measured sigh, she looked back at me. "I don't like your mutt." This made Knight growl loudly and I was worried he might get a boot to the face. But, Olivier stood, her nails retracted, and she gave me another hug with a slight glance towards the bite. "Do what I said. I'll do what I can to deter Arthur until you can break free. And when you do, keep running. Next time you see me, I hope you're not in trouble anymore." She jumped into the windowsill, then she turned back and grinned. "Oh. I almost forgot. Your evasion methods are impeccable. If I wasn't the one hunting you, they'd be chasing their tails for a century." Then she was gone.

"Nice friend," Knight commented dryly.

"She's an acquired taste."

"I have a feeling it takes a few centuries to acquire that particular taste." He sat up, popped his shoulders, and ran a hand through his long locks. "First things first." Smiling, he leaned in and stroked my cheek before kissing me slowly, like he was memorizing every inch of my mouth. Fuck, he was a good kisser. "And now..." No, more kisses. I pushed him back against the headboard, sat on his lap, and kissed him again, and again. "We should," he got out between kisses. "Lis, we should focus." I moved to his ear and I nibbled at the lobe before licking up the side while my fingers danced over the scars on his chest. "God damn it, woman. I am going to go insane."

I kissed him like he was the only man, or woman, I'd ever

kissed, and adjusted my spot on his cock until both of us gasped with pleasure.

"No sex," I breathed against his mouth. "I just want to hear you moan."

"*God*," he gasped, his hot breath only fueling my flame. Rocking ever so slowly, my clit bumped against his cock with every thrust of my hips. My panties and his shorts were the only things between us, and I wanted so badly to remove any barrier that stopped my skin from touching his. He was right, though. If we became lovers, our scent would change, and James would know.

A few orgasms wouldn't make a difference, and as much as Knight had teased me, it was my turn to tease him.

Clit against cock, bumping over and over. His hands found my hips and he increased my rhythm until I couldn't think, couldn't breathe. His moans were the hottest thing I'd ever heard. I wanted to listen to them for as long as possible. Every moan made me wetter, and every bump brought me closer.

Growling, he pushed us down until he was on top of me, and he picked up speed against my clit until I was breathless with need. He kissed me, taking the breath from my lungs so I gasped for more.

"Oh god," I moaned. "More, faster." I didn't think he could go faster, but he did, and my clit throbbed against him until I knew I was going to explode. "I'm going to..." He cut me off with a bruising kiss and brought his hands to my nipples, and I was gone. Waves of pleasure hit me and his screams announced his own orgasm, his hips moving slower and slower as we both came down. Wet and sweaty, all I could think was how much more I wanted from him. Our ragged breathing was the only sound in the room now, where moments before it was screams and moans.

"You think," I puffed against his neck. "You think Sara heard us?"

He laughed and rested his head against my shoulder. "We were pretty loud. She might've." Lifting his head, he stared at me with that brown puppy-eyed stare and kissed my bruised lips tenderly. "Fuck James and his fucking fuck face. He's keeping me from having you, and I hate him." He gathered me in his arms and sat us against the headboard again. "Sex is over, it's time to drink. I'll need some breakfast afterward. Not because I need it to grow new blood, I'm just hungry enough to eat my blanket. And maybe yours too." He moved his head to the side, exposing his neck.

I wanted to refuse his offer. I really did. I'd seen what the extra blood did to James, and it scared me. I didn't want to lose myself, but I was almost beyond caring. I was tired of being James's puppet. And drinking from Knight was the only way to be free.

"I'm scared," I told him. No use in hiding it. "You saw James. That's what happens when we drink more than once a day. We become like addicts. Except it's the power we crave. I'll become uncontrollable. And weird."

He kissed me and stroked my hair. "I won't let that happen."

I stared at his face, saw the determination he was trying to convey to me, and wished that it was true. "It will happen. It doesn't matter how much you try."

His eyes traveled around the room in thought and a muscle ticked in his jaw. "Okay. Then I'll monitor you. If I say you've had enough, then we stop. Agreed?" I nodded. As long as he could keep me in check, I could do this. "As much as I love having you in my lap, are we just going to sit here while my stomach rumbles?"

I bit into his neck quickly and his arms came up to cradle me like he'd done mere seconds before as he brought me to climax. I drank for a long time. Normal feedings only took about two minutes. I stayed on Knight's neck until my stomach started hurting from being so full, and my stomach can hold a lot of blood. He never pulled away. As soon as my teeth retracted, he slumped his head against my shoulder and brought his arms closer around me to hold me in place.

A knock at the door made us both jump.

20

GAINING STRENGTH

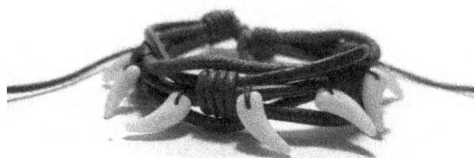

*B*REAKFAST!" Sara shouted in a sing-song tone. I got up from Knight's lap and he fell forward onto the comforter. When I opened the door, Sara had a cute look on her face like we'd been up to something during the night and she knew all about it.

She'd definitely heard us.

She was pushing a cart with a large tray full of food, enough food to feed a Lycan and a vampire, and then some. "Morning guests!" She pushed past me with the cart and rolled it over to the round table by my bed. The tray looked heavy, but she did her best to try and lift it until I had to go help her.

She'd literally cooked every kind of breakfast food there was, including the custard croissants I loved, and a few dishes I didn't recognize.

I smelled curry.

"There's plenty for both of you," she said with a cheerful smile. "He needs to keep up his strength. I mean both of you do. Silly me. Ta ta!" She waltzed out of the room, pushing the cart and humming something off-key.

"Well, she's cheerful today," Knight said with a chuckle.

"Get over here or I'm eating everything," I told him.

We ate. Well, I ate. He inhaled. He let me get my own food first, and after I filled my plate, he gobbled up everything else, including whatever smelled like curry. I felt slightly bad because I'd drunk so much from him. Though, I'd seen him eat this much before when he still had all of his blood.

He caught me staring at him. "Do you feel weird?" he inquired. I shook my head and leaned in for a kiss. If anything, I just felt more alert. Everything smelled crisper. I could hear better without pushing my senses out. I'd easily drunk three times more blood than I usually had every morning. "You can drink again before lunch, and you'll tell me if you start to feel different, right?" He was trying to help, but he was being a bit bossy.

"Okay, dad."

He narrowed his eyes. "I am not nearly old enough to be your dad, missy. Plus, that would be awkward considering I plan on seeing you naked in the near future." I chuckled and took another bite of the hash brown I'd been working on. "Speaking of which," he started. "Who are your parents? Aren't they going crazy with worry?"

"I don't know who they are," I said simply, my fork hovering in front of me. "Balthazar knows who my mother is, not that he'll ever tell me her name. My father is a nameless mystery. I don't even think about it."

Knight stared at me for a minute before putting some egg in his mouth. "Yes. I can see that you don't," he said around his food. "That's not normal, by the way."

"Fuck that. I'm a Born vampire. I don't have to be normal."

He snorted and blew a few pieces of egg onto the table. "Well," he continued after chewing and swallowing. "You're right about that." He sipped his second glass of orange juice. "Things like that tend to fade after a while, don't they?"

"It's not like I don't want to know who my father is," I admitted, though I'd never said that out loud to anyone. I never talked about my parents. Not even to Olivier. "It's just something I'll never get an answer for." He nodded like he understood. "Are other Lycans like you?" I regretted asking such a question, but I'd been wondering.

He looked hesitant. "You mean freaky with the moon or really, really old?"

"Immortal."

He almost didn't want to answer. I could see it on his face. "No. They aren't. Because I'm not like them. I was born human."

I was almost surprised to hear that, but I remembered that he was a werewolf. Werewolves were born human. "The scratches on your chest, they were from the Succubus."

"Yeah. They've never gone away. I spent time with a Lycan pack at first, just to learn about being one of them, until it was clear I wasn't one of them. I've been on my own ever since. I've never... seen another man like me. Not ever." I got up from my chair and sat on his lap to put my arms around him.

"It's because the Bicus are banned from changing or impregnating humans," I told him, and he rubbed my back with his free hand. "No one knows why, or those that do don't talk about it. If there were others like you, they'd be very old. Older than me."

This upset him greatly, though he tried to not show it. I tried to imagine what it would be like to have not a single soul that knew what it felt like to be what I am. I didn't like that mental image. And Knight was a pack animal. He'd never have a pack. Like an ant without a colony. A bee without a beehive.

Maybe I could be his beehive.

After Knight and I made out for a long time in the tub and we made sure I didn't smell like him, I went to my usual feeding at James's mansion. He didn't mention his proposal, probably trying to respect that I hadn't made up my mind yet. I drank from the human he provided, the extra blood only helping my cause. He wanted to talk about the merits of Napoleon, so I sat through that for over an hour.

Yawn.

He finally let me go before lunch. Drake took me home, and I fed from Knight again before Sara served us stewed duck. As I breathed in the smell of the food, I noticed everything smelled better. The colors of the 1950's kitchen were brighter like someone had turned up the graphics setting. I could hear every part of the hotel without having to focus my ears.

That night, with our underwear still on, Knight and I shared several life-shattering climaxes. With the extra blood in my system, I was almost afraid I would hurt him. I'd have to be very careful not to do so.

The next day came and I drank first from Knight, and then again from a human at James' house. When I came back, I had a lovely craving to take a walk. Knight's presence wasn't sitting well with the local populous, which was why we had been spending most of our time in the hotel before now, among other reasons. The humans had either never seen a Lycan, or had and didn't enjoy the memory. The vampires were no better.

"If they keep hissing at me, I'm going to be soaked in saliva by the end of the day," Knight complained after the fifth vampire had flashed their fangs in his direction.

In order for them to not tell James about us, we couldn't touch each other in public, and it was torturous. Still, I patted his arm like I would a puppy and sighed with happiness. I was so happy. Happy, happy, happy. "Don't worry. I'll protect you from the big bad vampires."

He glared at me frostily. "I can't tell if that's my blood talking or if you're just always like this. Oh, wait. You are." I stuck my tongue out at him and imagined kissing him against a telephone pole. "They say age makes you more mature, but in your case, they lied."

"Who said age makes you more mature?" I retorted. "I've never heard that. And I've been friends with plenty of philosophers."

"Like who, Friedrich Nietzsche?"

This time I glared. "Galileo, smarty pants."

He actually looked surprised. "Really? Wow. That's cool. I mean, I've known a few influential people too, but Galileo? What was he like?"

"And that is the question everyone always asks me. What was Tolkien like? Was Jane Austen cool? Did the pilgrims like music?"

He was trying not to laugh. "Did they?"

I shrugged and smiled. "I didn't know the pilgrims. The one person who asked me that, I lied and said no." He'd gone on to create an entire religion based around that fact, but let's not dredge up the past.

Knight was still on the topic of famous friends, and he just barely brushed his fingertips against mine, making flames flick up my arm. "Knowing someone who became famous isn't a frame of reference. You just knew them as a friend. You didn't know them as their public image."

"You sound rather knowledgeable," I told him, surprised

he understood something I'd felt for a long time. So many well-known people I'd called friend. And they were all dead now. Well, most of them. "Who'd you know?"

"I fought in the civil war, remember? I knew a lot of the officers. I met President Lincoln once. He smelled like shoe polish."

"What side did you fight on?" I'd already guessed, but I wanted to ask.

He smirked and looked away. "Not the side my family did, I can say that." We stopped at a hot dog stand to get some lunch. The owner, a young human, took one look at Knight and started to scowl.

"Sorry," he said curtly. "I don't want your business." Knight's face fell for a second before it went blank.

"Why not? We haven't done anything," I countered. I was James's main squeeze. All the humans should be doing whatever I wanted. Speaking of squeeze, I wondered how Knight would react if I pinched his luscious ass.

"My best friend is a vampire," the man spat. "Lycans killed her brother. James told everyone that this guy is a Lycan too. We don't want his kind around here."

I stared at the prejudice hot dog vendor, my mouth curled down and my good mood gone, until he looked me in the eye. "Please. We just want some hot dogs. We won't bother you anymore if you just give us some food."

To my surprise, he blinked, reached down, and handed me four hot dogs that were already prepared in a paper carton. Knight grabbed my elbow and tugged me away before the vendor could start complaining again.

"What the fuck just happened?" Knight asked when we'd turned the corner.

I knew exactly what had happened. I'd controlled the human. And I liked it.

21

I CONTROL YOU

*K*night wasn't happy. I handed him three of the hot dogs that he wolfed down, and I ate the other one while we walked. Once I was sure no one could see us, I pulled Knight into an alley and kissed him in between bites of hot dog.

I'd controlled someone's mind. It was a first for me. I wasn't sure what to think of it. On one hand, being controlled was horrid. Even in my current state, I remembered how it felt, though I had a hard time feeling sad about it. But on the other hand, I liked it. That hot dog man had been rude to my friend and I'd made him do what I wanted. That was a win in my book.

My kisses didn't distract him, and I looked up into his eyes, feeling only a tiny sliver of guilt. I didn't regret what I'd done. But I didn't want Knight to be mad at me.

"Eat your hot dog," was all he said.

I was still scared I'd made Knight mad. If he was mad, he wouldn't kiss me, and I liked it when he kissed me. Luckily, another drink from Knight before lunch took care of that for me. I no longer felt upset about what had happened, and I didn't care what Knight thought. I also wasn't totally feeling it when he started running his hands on my ass, but he stopped once he saw my disinterest.

We went downstairs to the kitchen, and Sara was there wearing green coveralls, her pink-tipped hair in two little buns.

"I'm about to start some falafels!" she said brightly, holding up a bowl of chickpea batter. I groaned and wished she would order pizza. Before, I'd found her odd taste in food quite charming. Now I just wanted her to stop being weird. Her face changed and she put the bowl back into the fridge. "On second thought, let's just order some pizza."

She trotted out of the room to get the hotel phone, leaving me in utter shock. Did I just influence her thoughts? Wicked!

Knight was equally surprised, but for a different reason. "I didn't know she liked pizza. I thought she hated it."

I needed to test this. I focused on where I knew Sara was standing in the other room and sent, "No mushrooms or peppers, extra meat, and breadsticks," to her.

She walked back into the kitchen and said, "I got extra meat, no mushrooms or peppers, and some breadsticks!"

That was the seal on my assumption. I'd influenced her thoughts. Knight was happy to get the pizza and didn't notice anything was off. I decided to not tell him what had happened. He'd just lecture me anyway. I didn't like lectures. I liked kisses.

After we ate, I drank from him again. I had to hold his arms to steady myself as a sonar pulse suddenly burst from my head. I knew where everyone in the town was without even thinking about it. I could tell their gender and smell their scent. It overwhelmed me and I whimpered slightly, wishing it would stop. Knight's fingers gently brushed through my hair.

"It's getting too much, isn't it," he asked me softly, his lips brushing over my neck.

I gasped and tightened my grip on him, willing myself to focus on only what I could see with my eyes. I lost a little of that giddy feeling I'd had before. "I have to keep going. I can handle it." My senses snapped back and the room became clearer. I could still sense everything at once, but it was dull, like a slight headache. "I just have to stay focused on my surroundings."

His hand slipped through my hair to rest on my shoulder, then lower to press me against him. "Remember, I'm here." I felt so warm and I wanted to feel him inside me. No more rubbing, no more underwear.

"We can't be intimate anymore," I groaned against him. "I'll go too far, it'll ruin everything."

His hands stilled, but he didn't pull away from me. "I understand."

By the next morning, I'd gone back to being giddy again and I wasn't upset about the lack of sexy times with Knight. When I went to James's, I truly had a full conversation with him without getting bored once. I still didn't want to stay here with him forever, but I couldn't remember why I didn't like being around him. I was careful to not act too weird, though. I didn't want him to know what I was up to. He checked his bite again, and despite the enormous amount of blood in my system, it hadn't faded. Not even a little.

On the way back to the hotel with Drake, I chatted him up with questions about his parents, which was completely inappropriate, but I didn't care. I even mentioned how he was not-human and human at the same time, and that it weirded me out. He ignored me.

Poo on you, Drake. I don't need to know your secret. It's probably boring anyway. Like you. You don't even go by your real name.

Knight isn't boring. Knight tastes good. He makes me laugh, and gives me beautiful pleasure. I might keep him. Provided he stops being such a Debbie Downer all the time.

My mind control powers worked on every human. They

didn't work on Knight. Maybe it was a werewolf thing, or maybe I just didn't want to control him.

He was so fucking bossy. We went to the movies after I'd been bingeing on his blood for almost a week. I wanted to control the humans serving food, but noooo, he told me to stop talking and stand in the corner like a little toddler that had stolen cookies. He paid for the food, like a moron. I could've saved him ten bucks, but whatever. His loss. He also wouldn't let me take someone else's seat. It's not my fault that the seats I wanted were already occupied!

"There are 32 people in here," I informed him once we'd settled in our seats and I'd stolen the popcorn from him. He grabbed a few handfuls when I was distracted by the smells and sounds in the room.

"Fascinating," was his response. Humph. He can't even appreciate how awesome my powers are. What good are you? You're supposed to be impressed. Cameron would be impressed. He'd be like, ooo Lisbeth, you're so awesome, like some superhero I forgot the name of. I needed a cape. People with powers have capes.

"Stop talking out loud or I'm going to spank you," Knight bossed. Like I said, so bossy. The spanking sounded nice though. "I am not bossy," he added. Oh. I was talking out loud again. I stuffed my mouth full of popcorn before I could reveal the location to my secret superhero bunker.

22

I SMELL FUDGE

*T*he next day, I could feel the emotions of everyone near me. Sara enjoyed the taste of guacamole far too much. James thought my smile was pretty, but he also thought windows were too flat. The ice cream man hated the smell of dairy. And Knight. He was worried about me. So worried. Also annoyed that my internal monologue kept spilling out of my mouth, and most of it was about how fluffy cotton candy was. I patted his cheek and told him to stop fussing over me, and also to learn to appreciate fluffy things.

Knight and I had started at three feedings per day. Then four. Then five. By the time we were up to six times per day, it had been almost two weeks, and the giddiness I'd felt at first was gone. Now I just felt powerful. Sara automatically cooked foods I wanted. No one in town charged me for anything. Men didn't flirt with me. Women didn't stare at Knight. And James. Dear James. Seeing him was easy. His bite was still there, but even though I'd grown considerably stronger, it wasn't enough to tip him off. Or I'd just gained the ability to fool him.

But the cost. The cost of the blood binge was starting. I became short-tempered if someone messed up what I'd asked for. Sara had a constant stomachache from the rich food I enjoyed. I didn't care about anyone's feelings. I was the only one that mattered, including with Knight. We barely touched anymore, and I missed it so desperately that at every turn I was prepared to tear his clothes off to have him back in my arms.

I'd reached that level of power that I feared so badly. I was uncontrollable and unstoppable. And I wasn't afraid of it anymore. I liked it. I wanted more. I never wanted to come down. With this much power, I could stop Arthur and the Hunters. I'd be free. Maybe I'd start my own little town somewhere with nice humans to do my bidding and Knight in my bed. With my powers, I'd be able to tell exactly what they were doing at any moment of the day. There'd be no crime, no insurgency, only me and my whims. And they would all obey me. I had no doubt about that.

Knight questioned me every day to check on my mental state. I knew he could tell I was getting worse, so I had trouble understanding why he kept bothering me with the constant questions. The irrational part of my brain that was taking over didn't want to care what he thought about all of it, but somehow, I still did. When he got mad at me, I felt sad, and all I wanted was for him to forget whatever I did to anger him and say he liked me again. I hated upsetting him. Even so, it didn't make me stop. Not even a little.

On day fifteen, I'd decided to stop humoring him and his little checklist.

"Enough," I told him. We were sitting in my hotel room, and he was trying to ask his daily routine of questions. "This is stupid. I'm fine. It's time for more blood." I didn't crave the blood, no. I wanted more power. I wanted to reach into the sky and bring the stars down.

He ignored my complaints, so I got up from the floor and sat down on his lap. We hadn't been that close in days, and he didn't even react, he just shifted so it was more comfortable. No phone in his pocket, no sir-ee. He did not have a boner for me.

"Okay, next question. Is your tongue numb?"

I traced his jugular with my finger and thought about licking it. "Nope."

"Do you smell fudge when there is no fudge?"

I rolled my eyes. "Have you always been such a nerd?"

"Answer."

I planted a long lick on his neck. "The grocery store down the street has some fudge bars for sale, they smell good. Other than that, no."

"Stop licking me," he ordered. I still couldn't control him. I'd dismissed it as a wolf thing, but sometimes I tried just for fun. Make mad passionate sex to me. Sexxxx. Nope. He stood up, carried me to the bed, and sat back down on the edge of it. I could've drunk from him in the chair, but he preferred the bed so he could collapse on it if he needed to. I also preferred the bed, but not for drinking. "Drink. I'll ask the questions later."

I sunk my teeth into his neck and oh my fucking god did it taste good. His blood was the best I'd ever had. Other blood tasted too salty or like a cup of dishwater. His was like honey wine, deeply satisfying and crisp. Crispy blood. More crispy blood. Maybe when I was done feeding, he'd touch me again. I so wanted him to touch me.

"Lis..." his voice was strained and his hands gripped my rib cage tightly. What did he want? I was busy. "Lis please," he begged. I liked begging. Maybe he'd have sex with me now.

Something clicked in my head and I registered what was happening.

I was draining him.

I shrieked in horror and pulled away. His body slumped down onto the bed and he struggled to breathe. I'd drunken so much of his blood. Clarity slapped into me and I felt my body go cold like someone had dumped ice water on my head.

"Knight!" I screamed. His hand reached up and he took mine, squeezed it, and then he closed his eyes.

It took Knight over an hour to recover. I felt his heart almost stop once, but his body worked quickly to keep him from dying. He held my hand the entire time, squeezing it like it gave him strength. When he could finally sit up, I threw myself into his arms and started crying.

"I almost killed you," I sobbed into his shirt. His arms went around me and he held me close.

"I know," he soothed. "But to be fair, I almost killed you once."

I beat a fist against his chest. "You should've stopped me!" I was talking about me almost draining him, but I also meant everything else. He should've stopped me. He promised me he would. And he didn't.

We sat like that for a long time. I could feel every muscle in his body, every sinew, every intake of breath. It was all too much. The smells, the sounds, the emotions. I started to sob and grab my head.

"Knight," I whimpered, his hands coming up to hold me closer to him. "This is too much. It's my limit. I can't do this anymore." The overflow of Knight's blood was working through my system and I started to get flashes of things going on around town. Make it stop. Please make it stop. In the midst of it all, I felt something snap. The hold James had over me dissolved, and the bite on my neck slowly closed over. I was free.

I passed out.

When I woke up the next morning, Knight was sitting next to me on the bed eating a bowl of kimchi and eggs, watching something on the flat screen tv about the Civil War. One of my many orders to Sara had been buying a tv. He saw me stir, so he handed me a glass of water he'd had waiting for me.

"Morning," he greeted around a mouthful of food. I took the water and downed it in long gulps.

I wiped my mouth on my sleeve when I'd emptied the glass. "Are you okay?"

"I'm fine," he said simply. He went back to watching the tv, so I put a hand on his knee, drawing his eyes up to my face.

"Knight," I said slowly. "You didn't stop me. You promised me you would. And you didn't." I felt tears form and roll down my cheeks. "I went into this trusting that you'd be there to pull me out of it. I was there. I was on the precipice, and you let me go over." I knew blaming him wasn't entirely fair, but I couldn't help it. I'd been so scared seeing him almost die. And I couldn't shoulder that blame on my own, or I'd never be able to live with what I'd done.

He set his bowl down on the nightstand and folded me into his arms without hesitation, stroking my hair and tucking a few strands behind my ear with his fingers. "Lis. I'm sorry. I'm so sorry. I know you trusted me, and I broke that trust. I'm so sorry," he repeated, and I heard tears in his voice, but I couldn't see past the droplets in my eyes. "You couldn't see yourself like I did. Pulling you back wouldn't have worked. Not with how far you were gone. Sara and I talked it over. I had to let you almost kill me. It was the only way to bring you out." He sniffed and tears spilled onto his shirt. "I'm so sorry."

I was in the only place I felt safe anymore, in Knight's gentle and strong embrace. We both cried. He cried because he knew how much he'd hurt me, and how he'd broken my trust. I cried because I'd never felt so scared in all my long life. What if I had killed him? I would've still been high on blood, and there's no telling what crazy notion would've gone through my head. Maybe I would've tracked down and killed the Hunters. Or run away to start my own slave town. Or maybe I would've killed James and kept this town for myself. If I had killed Knight, no one could've stopped me.

If I'd killed him, I would've lost what we had growing between us. The fevered kisses, the passion, the... love. He would've never known how I felt about him. Maybe I didn't even know, but that didn't matter. What I'd become, and the things I'd done, even the things I hadn't done but wanted to. It violated almost every moral code I had. I felt so ashamed. I wanted to die from the shame.

Knight was my lifeboat now. I clung to him until I ran out of tears. He'd long since stopped crying and was gently stroking my long brown locks. We'd been silent for several hours, just sitting there together, until he spoke.

"I'm sorry I left you."

"What?" I asked in genuine confusion.

"When I shifted and attacked you. I was so mortified at

what I'd done. I know I can't control myself when I'm shifted, but... I was still ashamed. I hurt you. I'm supposed to protect you."

"Because of the bracelet, right?" Somehow, I was let down at the thought, and I tried not to think of why that was. Before he could answer, I remembered I'd broken James's hold on me the night before and I pulled away from Knight to sit back on my heels. "Wait, why haven't we left yet? James will know I'm not under his control anymore. He'll come after us and bite me again, and all of this will have been useless."

Knight wasn't concerned, and automatically he reached out for me to sit back in his arms. "Sara's handling him right now. He's too focused on her list of complaints to be bothered with you for the moment. We needed time to recover." Staying where I was, I felt Sara at James's house and the turmoil of emotions going on there, most of which were coming from her. He was truly occupied.

"Are we... okay?" Knight asked me. I doubted he meant in the feeling okay kind of way. As an answer, I swept him up in a passionate kiss. A kiss that I'd almost lost forever, and I hugged him so close to me, I felt as if we would meld together.

23

A VISIBLE SCAR

The enormous amount of extra blood in my system was making my head pulse with every heartbeat, and every pulse brought random information about the town around me. People were fighting, loving, eating, and walking their dogs. It was hard to focus on getting packed, but every time I stopped moving, Knight would bring me close for a kiss.

Thanks to Sara, Excalibur had been sitting in her garage this entire time. We loaded it up with our bags and Knight drove us out of town. We didn't talk much. It had been a very long seven weeks. The longest of our lives. I couldn't help but wonder if we'd ever recover from it all. I didn't have high hopes on the matter.

The further we got from the town, the fewer people I

sensed, until I could only feel Knight. He was tired. Sad. Angry. Hungry. And relieved. So relieved that we'd gotten away. But he was scared. Scared for me, and how I would come out of this. I tried not to delve into anything related to me in his feelings, as curious as I was. I'd already violated too many boundaries.

"Hey," I told him drowsily, my sleepy state keeping me from blocking out my powers. "In the interest of full disclosure, I can still feel your emotions. But don't worry. I'm not going to invade your privacy. All your secret thoughts are safe. But don't focus on them too strongly or I'll feel them."

He nodded and smiled slightly. "Good to know." I leaned against his warm shoulder and shut my eyes. "Lis," he whispered above my head. "Thank you for telling me that."

"Least I could do," I mumbled. "Since I'm such a horrible person now." I drifted off to the rhythmic thumping of Knight's heartbeat, and slept until he pulled into a motel and got us a room.

The room smelled like air conditioner and carpet fibers. I shuffled over to the bed, flopping down on my stomach with my cheek pressed against the scratchy comforter. My head pounded, my stomach rolling so hard it was going to go out the door. My body was used to having several pints of new blood every day, and it was not pleased that I hadn't drunk since the night before.

Knight sat down next to me and studied me carefully, no doubt wondering if he needed to bring over one of the trashcans in case I needed to hurl. "Withdrawal?" he asked. I nodded. I felt horrible.

"I've wanted to die several times recently," I groaned. "But right now... I really, really, fucking want to."

"Tomorrow will be worse," he said, not even trying to sugar coat it. I glared at him. Whatever else I could say about him, he never babied me.

I finally fell asleep after sharing a pizza with Knight and it didn't come back up. I drifted straight into nightmares. My dreams took me back to James's town, forcing me to relive the pain and agony I'd felt under his control. I woke up sweaty and shaking. My hand automatically went to where James's bite had been. Careful to not disturb Knight sleeping beside me, I got up and went to the large mirror on the hotel closet door. The bite was still gone, with only a light red mark to indicate it had ever been there.

It was the only scar I had that was visible.

I was still running my fingers over the scar and wondering how my life had come to this moment when I smelled lilacs. Balthazar was behind me when I looked up, and I turned to fall into his arms.

"Where have you been, you ass!" I sobbed into his dark blue suit. His hands came around me and he hugged me close.

"My apologies," he said softly. "I couldn't help you, and I thought my presence might distress you even more." He was right. I couldn't bear the thought of him seeing me drunk on blood and power.

I softly pounded my fists on his chest and whispered, "ass," for good measure. He kissed the top of my head, ignoring my weak tirade.

"You've still got the dog, I see," he noted with disapproval.

I smiled against his coat. "He came back for me. He stayed with me and helped me escape." Also, he sexed me up without actually sexing me up. That part was the best.

"He's a dog. He shouldn't want to be within ten feet of you." Balthazar let me go and turned to study the sleeping werewolf. "Does he have feelings for you?"

All of the passion between us came to mind, but he'd never mentioned feelings. "Why would you think that?" I put a hand to my temple as my headache suddenly became apparent.

"Boys fall for girls," Balthazar said simply, like it was a no-brainer.

"You're ridiculous." I poured myself a glass of water and gulped most of it down.

The Incubus rolled his shoulders in a shrug, and continued studying Knight's still form. "Your blood count is high. You could see his feelings for you. Easily."

"You can tell?" Balthazar nodded, his face showing what I could only call... jealousy? "No, I won't do that. He knows I can delve into his mind, and I promised him I wouldn't." That made me smile. Not the promise part, the fact that I hadn't lost my clarity, even though my body was raging with powers. Balthazar made a humph noise and tapped his cane against his shoe.

"I can see his feelings," he declared, tossing his black hair back. "Would you like to know?"

I won't lie. I was tempted. Knight was asleep, and he'd never know, but I was done with acting like that. Never again.

I shook my head, crossing my arms firmly over my chest. "No. I promised him that his secrets were safe. And anyway, it doesn't matter. Why would he love a vampire? He's a were-wolf." I was making excuses. Feeble ones, at that.

"Stranger things have happened," Balthazar noted.

Maybe I could've hoped for more from Knight, but I felt like shit, and I wasn't in the mood to wonder. Balthazar left and I went back to sleep against Knight's warm back.

Knight was right. I did feel a hundred times worse the next day. Lifting my head from my pillow, every movement causing complete agony. My lips groaned before I could stop them.

"That bad, huh?" Knight commented from behind me. I sat up and blinked a few times. My head hurt so badly, it was hard to make them focus on anything. I could barely see Knight across the room. He was sitting at the little table by the window, eating breakfast. He'd kept the lights off and shut the curtains, which I greatly appreciated. I couldn't handle bright light right then. I swung my legs over the edge of the bed, planted my feet on the carpet, and stood up. My legs instantly gave way underneath me. "Hey, life alert, stop playing around." Despite his jibs, he got up from his chair, but I motioned for him to stay. I needed to do this on my own. "I happen to like your face, please don't break it." I pulled myself up and forced my legs to support my weight. They wobbled a few times, but I managed to make it to the other chair at the table before they gave out again. "You okay?" I nodded. Sitting on the table was a plastic box with croissants and some pudding cups. I looked at it and up at Knight. He grinned and shrugged. "I can't make custard croissants. This is the next best thing." He served me up an opened pudding cup and a croissant on a paper plate, before breaking off a piece of croissant and dipping it in the pudding. "Here, try." I felt my lip tremble. He'd really tried to make going through this a little bit easier by making his own version of my favorite food. I didn't deserve him, him or his love. He suddenly pointed a finger in my face to distract me. "No. No tears. Eat the pastry."

I reached out to take the small bite of food. My hands shook and I couldn't keep it in my grip. It fell into my lap, smearing my shirt with pudding. "Sorry," I apologized softly. He clicked his tongue, broke off another bit, dipped it, and held it up to my mouth. "Now you're feeding me?" He ignored my protest and shoved the bite in while I was talking.

Fuck, it was good.

"Is that French vanilla?" I asked with the pastry in my mouth. He nodded and broke off another bite. The second bite made my head pound as my senses tried to inform me how amazing it smelled. I lost control for a few seconds, but that was all my powers needed. I could see, hear, smell, and taste everything nearby. There were four other humans in hotel rooms and two in the office. One was walking outside with a cart that smelled like cleaning products. Her breath smelled like chocolate.

"Hey," Knight soothed. He took my head in his hands and kissed my forehead gently. "Focus, okay?" Gripping his wrist in my hand, I grounded myself with the scent of his hair. His shampoo smelled like cinnamon. I took a deep breath and regained control.

I looked up at him feebly as he ran a hand through my hair. "Why are you still here?" I expected... well, I wasn't sure what I expected. The bracelet promise, maybe. Because we're kind of lovers, even if I'd been pushing him away for weeks. He doesn't have anywhere else to go. I have money, maybe.

But that wasn't what he answered. He stared into my eyes and said, "Where else would I be?"

I plunged forward and kissed him, but the pain in my head throbbed with every movement. "Oww," I said between kisses. "Oww, oh god, it hurts."

"There's no rush," he promised and kissed me again before pulling me into his lap. "There's plenty of time for that. You need to get better."

So. Knight and I had to make a new plan now. Something long term. And something that involved both of us. I knew there was nowhere I could go, anywhere on the globe, that would stop the Hunters from finding me. I'd be on the run forever. But, with Knight at my side, it would be a life I wanted to live.

Our first pit-stop was going back to Jesse's pack. He'd called us during my detox and said he could get us a car that couldn't be tracked by the Hunters. He sounded as if there was more besides the car for his reason to call us, but he didn't elaborate.

A week of detox, which did involve some throwing up, had mostly gotten me back to normal power levels. The pain and shakes had subsided, and I was back to needing Knight's blood every morning, which he provided without complaint or fear. I felt strong again, and absolutely in control over my powers.

Despite my recovery, I still had nightmares about James. Being around too many people scared me now. I was so afraid he'd be around the corner, ready to bite me again and steal my freedom. Knight said I had PTSD, a human disorder. I told him I wasn't human. Still, I stayed in the hotel room while he packed Excalibur up with our bags. I came outside after carefully pushing out my senses and making sure no one else was nearby. It was safe.

Knight drove, even though he was practically bent in half

in my tiny car. I would miss my Excalibur, but I would gladly sacrifice it to keep us safe. I unbuckled, laying my head on his lap while we drove, and he kept his spare hand on me, stroking my cheek gently.

Jesse's pack lived in a trailer park on the edge of a forest. Perfect for Lycans to run all they wanted. We pulled up in their non-paved road. All the trailers were parked in a large semi-circle, leaving a big clearing for all the Lycans to gather in. They had grills, picnic tables, a basketball hoop, and still had enough room to spare.

The pups were wrestling in the open space around the trailers, desperate to work off their raging hormones and prove themselves. Rather than stopping it, the adults were egging them on while cooking something on a grill for lunch.

I waited to get out of the car after Knight was out and near my door. There were so many people here. I hated how scared I was. When I stepped out onto the trodden grass, Knight reached for me the same moment I brought a hand up to clutch his arm.

"We'll leave soon," he promised, rubbing my shoulder. I tried to focus only on the smell of the barbecued meat. It was mouthwatering.

Jesse's trailer was at the head of the area. It was decorated with Halloween decorations and a large red flag with a paw print on it. His mate sat on the small wooden front porch, snapping green beans. I could sense him inside the trailer.

"Hey Toni," Knight said to the Alpha female. "Jesse here?"

I whispered, "He's inside" at the exact moment she said it out loud.

Jesse came out, hearing us, and smiled a smile that didn't quite reach his eyes. "Knight." He glanced at me and the smile faded when he saw Knight's arm around me. "You're here for the car?" Knight nodded. "It's waiting for you, but you don't have to rush off. Stay for lunch."

"We appreciate the offer, but we have to get going," Knight told him. Jesse gestured to Toni, who understood his wordless cue and stood up, going inside the trailer to rummage through the fridge for something before she came back with a foil package. She tossed a small object to Knight and he caught it without looking. Car keys. She pitched the foil to me, but I flinched and cowered behind Knight, so he caught it and handed it to me. It smelled like brisket.

He threw her the keys to Excalibur and motioned to my tiny car. "You can keep it." Considering she, and most of their pack, drove motorcycles, I wasn't sure if she'd like my little economy car. They'd probably sell it. Or Balthazar would steal it again.

"She okay?" Jesse asked, showing genuine concern for the way I was behaving. I was a powerful vampire and I was hiding behind a werewolf. I really had to get this under control. I took a deep breath and stepped away from Knight.

"I'm good," I assured him. And I knew I would be. Eventually.

"Sorry you can't stay," Jesse said, his face looking more and more pinched. He meant it, but I could feel something off with him. Knight stiffened, feeling it too, and quickly said his farewells before leading me to the car they'd gotten for us. It was a teal convertible. Knight didn't even pause before dumping our bags into it. As scared as I still was, despite trying not to be, I was able to turn my nose up at the color.

"Teal?" I commented when we'd driven away. "Couldn't have picked something nicer like sea foam?"

"He didn't consult a color expert, I guess," Knight teased, but then he sobered, his fingers gripping the steering wheel firmly. "That was weird. He offered for us to stay but... I could sense he was just being polite about it."

I wanted to mention that they probably didn't like seeing a werewolf with his arm around a vampire, but my eyes went to the glove compartment. Someone had added a little sticker of a vampire smiley face right next to the press handle. Why would Jesse put that there? Maybe it had been there when they bought it? I opened the compartment and found a letter on top of some maps.

It was addressed to me.

I shut the compartment quickly, and leaned back against my seat before Knight could notice what I was doing. Instead, he poked the foil package in my lap.

"That smells good. They were nice to give it to us."

"I made her do it. I reached inside and I said, brisket, woman!" He knew I couldn't do that anymore, so I hoped he knew I was trying to be funny.

He snorted and poked me in the side. "Let me have some and I'll let it pass."

"You are mistaken. She gave this to me. Not you. Find your own brisket."

"Hey, I gave you my lifeblood. I am entitled. Now give." He tried to swipe it from me, so we played keep away until I decided to open it before he could tear the foil and get brisket everywhere.

THE HUNTER RETURNS

I didn't read the letter until we'd checked into a hotel before nightfall and Knight left to go swimming. After checking him out for several breathtaking minutes, I paid close attention to his position in the courtyard with my now normal level of powers while I retrieved the envelope from the glove compartment. I opened it to find a letter written by Jesse.

⚔

Lisbeth,

Knight isn't safe. He stayed with my pack for a few days last month, and in that short amount of time, everyone could tell he was different. It caused a stir among us.

You must understand. He's the true form of our species, one of the Primal werewolves. They are dangerous and uncontrollable when the moon has them in her grasp, no matter what they're like during the day.

I know he's a good man since he's chosen to protect you. It didn't matter what I said to them, a few in my pack were too afraid of him. They told others that a Primal werewolf has been found. I banished them from the pack, but the damage was done. The Lycan elders have dispatched packs to find Knight.

I don't know what they'll do to him if he's captured. I ask you to protect him like he's protected you. Make sure they don't find him. I have to believe he's not dangerous, as I hope you do too.

Jesse

I stared at the page for a long time, the words boring holes into me. Now Knight was being hunted too, and would most likely be executed if they caught him. I felt him get out of the pool, so I left the car and walked to where he stood, toweling himself off. I stared at the water drops that floated down the five pink scratches on his chest.

Drool pooled in my mouth and I wanted to taste those droplets.

"What's up?" he said when he saw me. "You look serious. And sexy." I handed him the letter. I didn't care if Jesse thought I should keep it secret. I wouldn't hide anything from Knight. Not now. Not after all we'd been through. He took it, started reading, and slowly lowered himself to the nearest pool chair. Sighing, he handed it back when he was finished, his eyes staring at the concrete by his feet. "Why'd you let me read that? You could have just told me the gist of it."

"Full disclosure," I reminded him. But there was something else. He'd been rejected by his own kind so much, and Jesse had treated him with kindness. "And also, I didn't want you to think Jesse doesn't like you."

His gaze softened when he looked up at me. "Thank you. That was kind." Sighing, he looked away at the wet concrete around the pool. "Now I'm being hunted too. And not for breaking rules. Just for who I am. That's comforting." He stood up and grabbed his towel, slinging it over his shoulder, he took hold of my neck and kissed me enough that I wanted to rip both our clothes off. "It's the full moon tonight," he breathed against my lips. "I'm going into the forest until dawn. Stay here and wait, please?"

Begrudgingly, I agreed. After we went back to our room, he took his room key and a change of clothes in case his current outfit was ruined in the shift. After he left, I couldn't sleep. Between the nightmares about James, and the constant worry he'd somehow find me, I could only rest when I was too exhausted to keep my eyes open. I watched history specials until the only thing playing was infomercials. So I watched those too.

At almost 7 am, I was still awake when the hotel door opened and Knight stumbled in wearing the change of clothes he'd brought. He was favoring one leg, and had a nasty red scratch on his collarbone. His breath came in ragged puffs. Without speaking, he walked over to the bed I was sitting on and collapsed next to me, and within seconds I heard snoring.

He slept past noon so I had to renew our hotel reservation for another night, whether or not we would stay that long. I was munching some cereal I'd snagged at the free hotel breakfast, and watching something about King Tutankhamen when Knight finally stirred. He sat up, wiped his mouth, and stretched until his back and shoulders popped. His eyes looked like he had a hangover, but the mark on his collarbone was healed and his leg was fine when he stood up. Kissing me once, he went to the bathroom for a shower, and came back in by the time I'd finished my cereal. I was trying not to stare at him, but he noticed me peeking glances.

"I know," he said. "I look like shit. It happens. And I have a few more days until it's over so, you know, yay." He tossed himself into one of the chairs and leaned his head back. "Did you sleep?" I shook my head. I was tired, but I wasn't to the point of collapsing yet.

"Do you remember anything when you're shifted?" I asked him.

He shrugged. "Bits and pieces. Mostly just the things I kill. I always kill something. For sport I guess. I don't eat it or anything. I just kill it." He scrubbed a hand down his face. "I don't know if Jesse is right. I don't know if I'm good. Maybe there's a reason there's no one else like me. The Lycans obviously don't like a Primal werewolf existing. Maybe I am a goddamn monster."

The bed creaked when I got up, and I walked over to put my arm around his shoulders, running my hand up his arm to soothe him. "It's just fear. Fear makes us do stupid things. Take the Salem witch trials, for example." I was trying to lighten the mood, but it didn't work. Knight stayed pensive and distant after that. He even made me drive the convertible, which made me a nervous wreck for the first hour.

When night rolled around, he left me at the truck stop I'd picked for us to sleep at. I had no intention of staying in the car waiting for dawn to arrive. I locked the car doors and hoped no one would bother it before following Knight across the parking lot. He walked far into the forest until he reached a clearing that let in the light from the stars. He set his change of clothes on the ground and walked far away from them before he sat down to wait for the moon to rise.

It took over twenty minutes for the moon to reach its zenith, and he was fine until the beams of ghostly light fell on him. He didn't have time to remove his clothes before they were shredded when his body started growing. As before, his hands became claws, his face contorted into a snout, and every inch of his skin grew hair as his muscles grew. I was prepared for his scent turning acrid, but this time it wasn't quite as unpleasant as it had been the first time. The Primal werewolf howled at the moon in a long mournful breath and sped off into the forest.

Following him was easy. I ran for the first time in

months, and even though my powers were back to normal, I'd somehow retained a higher level of senses. I knew that there was a family of six rabbits asleep in a burrow five trees over. A herd of twenty-three deer half a mile to the right. Squirrels sleeping in trees, birds in their nests. Bats, owls, raccoons, mice.

The sounds and images were overwhelming me, and I started having a panic attack. I stopped following Knight and rested for a minute, slowing my rapid heartbeat and gasping for air. If I focused on him alone, I could make myself ignore everything else. I closed my eyes and found Knight running and jumping to grab tree branches so he could swing on them. That was weird. Taking a deep breath, I focused as hard as I could, and everything except him fell away. I started running again.

I followed him for hours, always making sure to stay downwind so he wouldn't catch my scent. Oddly enough, he was acting like a kid at the playground. He growled if any animal got too close to him, but he never hurt them. Was this really the werewolf who had sliced me open with one swipe?

Everything was going fine until we passed a river and a group of wild dogs came into scent range. Knight caught their smell and his elongated ears perked to the direction it was coming from. He growled, but didn't charge in their direction. Instead, he turned to go the other way. It was too late. The dogs had caught the scent of a wolf in their territory. They growled, yipped, and barked, and then they came after him. The dogs were small in comparison, but they knew how pack rules went. He was alone. There was no pack to help him, and he had trespassed in their home.

They charged.

I wanted to help him. If he hadn't attacked me the first time, I would have bust in and tore those dogs to pieces, but I had to watch from a distance. The Alpha, a large German shepherd, tore into Knight's leg, but his skin was too tough for the dog to break. That didn't stop the big dog from trying. The other dogs did the same, so Knight fought back. He swiped a hand at them, slinging them away from him. The ones he'd hit whimpered and staggered off to lick their wounds. As focused as I was on him, I could tell he wasn't doing this for enjoyment or sport. He had attacked them back to protect himself. It was fucking magnificent to watch. He was beautiful and powerful.

Knight clawed the Alpha off his leg and the dog's body flopped to the ground where it stopped moving. Their Alpha dead, the other dogs ran away as quickly as they could. Knight heaved, whimpered, and put a clawed hand over his leg. It was slightly pink from the dog's teeth, but it wasn't bleeding. He jumped up and started running again. I lifted a leg to follow when something grabbed me from behind.

"Lisbeth," said a voice from above my head. "I'm so glad I've finally found you."

Fuck. Me.

It was Arthur.

I considered running. I really did. But I couldn't. Knight was far enough ahead of us that Arthur with his limited senses hadn't seen or smelled him, I hoped, and if I ran, Knight might be seen. Even if I was caught, Knight would be safe as long as the Lycans didn't find him. That's all that mattered to me, keeping Knight safe.

"You are one hard vampire to find, my lady," Arthur observed, his hold on me very tight. He rummaged through his pocket for something, keeping a knife pressed to my spine. When he found what he was looking for –handcuffs– he slapped them on my wrists. They were made for vampires, so tugging on them did no good. He turned me around and clicked a padlock and chain onto the handcuffs, a chain that was connected to his belt also via padlock. I didn't put too much hope in finding the keys.

I looked up into his icy blue eyes and scowled at him. "And you're one persistent fuck."

"After you," he said gallantly, and gestured to the direction he wanted me to walk. I dutifully went, trying not to glance back at Knight. "Funny," Arthur commented when we'd been walking for a few minutes. "After how hard you tried to evade me, I thought you'd give up a fight when I caught you." 'When' he'd said. Not 'if'. He was nothing if not egotistical. Why had I ever thought he was attractive? Not that he could *ever* hold a candle to Knight. "And I never expected you to be just standing there either. Are you that short on blood that you couldn't sense me?"

Why did he care? He'd caught his quarry. Job well done.

Maybe he liked gloating. Or maybe he didn't like catching his prize so easily. Either way, he was a buttmunching asswipe.

This fucker prattled the whole way back, and loudly. It wasn't typical for him. Back at the Order, the most words I'd ever heard him say was the conversation we'd had at the chessboard.

"Is there a reason you won't shut the fuck up?" I finally asked him.

"Never you mind," was his response. Lovely.

We finally reached the abandoned building the Hunters were staying at, after a good thirty minutes of hiking. Arthur marched me through the old rusted doors, past two Hunters guarding them. A warehouse opened before me, and I was surrounded by Hunters. There had to be over two dozen of them, and each one as cold, ruthless, and slightly scary looking as Arthur was. My senses informed me of their exact number, twenty-nine, and how many weapons they all had, over two hundred collectively.

That was a tad overkill. I mean, I was awesome, no doubt. But I was just a single vampire.

"Well damn," I commented as Arthur put a hand to my back to shove me forward. "I wasn't aware I was this danger-ous. Maybe I should've gotten a tattoo to look scarier. Oww, fuck!" Arthur had shoved me again, hard, and tugged on the chain to stop me from falling, but it made the cuffs dig into my wrists.

"That's enough, Arthur," a clear, stern voice said. I knew

that voice. Olivier walked through the ranks as they parted for her. Her tight steampunk dreads perfectly match her leather Hunter garb, which included a leather bikini. She had seven weapons on her person, and I could only see four of them. Her face looked hard as she turned to me. She breathed in a heavy sigh, but other than that, she had no reaction. This wasn't my best friend. This was Olivier the Hunter, and fuck was she hot. She was more terrifying than everyone else in the room. Blinking, she looked back at Arthur. "We've got her. Now let's go. The Council has convened in New York, and we need to get her there as fast as possible."

Arthur held up a hand. "Not just yet. I have some extra business here. In the meantime, let's lock her–"

Arthur was interrupted by a loud crash as the warehouse doors burst open. It was Knight, still shifted, swinging his paws at the guards. His claws hit deeply and the guards fell. He turned to see the large group of Hunters surrounding him and roared in fearless challenge. The other Hunters sprang into action, unsheathing swords and cocking guns, and Arthur grabbed my arm so hard his long nails cut into me. I cried out, just slightly at the unexpected pain, and drew Knight's attention to me. He charged through the Hunters, clawing and throwing until he reached me.

"Well," Arthur started saying, no doubt about to monologue. Knight brought his claws down to the chain that tied me to Arthur, and it snapped in half, the force knocking me to the floor. With his other hand, he smacked Arthur so hard the warrior went flying.

Knight stood over me in a protective stance, his teeth bared, and with a loud growl he dared them to challenge him. He'd done massive damage to the other Hunters. Vampires didn't heal quickly when a werewolf or Lycan was the attacker. I smelled blood everywhere. Knight looked down at me, and I felt a twinge of fear that he would attack me as well. Instead, he gently reached down to hook my cuffs with a claw and huffed at Olivier in signal to unlock them. She grabbed the keys from Arthur, whose stupidly hot face had a red slice from cheek to forehead from Knight's claws. Olivier freed me, giving my hand a slight squeeze as she did, and backed away.

I stood, and Knight knelt with his back to me. He motioned with a claw and grunted. *Get on my back.* I mounted his back, he grabbed my legs tightly, and we sprinted out of the warehouse.

25

CONFESSIONS AT DAWN

night ran and ran, his claws never slacking on their grip around my legs. I clutched his neck tightly, my face buried in his furry neck. He took us away from the car and our things. None of that mattered now. If the Hunters found him, they'd take him to the Lycans, and he would be killed. I couldn't let that happen. I wouldn't. I didn't care what I had to do to keep him safe, nothing was more important to me than him staying alive.

Knight didn't stop running until dawn. When the moon disappeared from the sky, he stumbled, throwing me from his back, and knelt on the ground in pain. Whimpering, his body started shifting back to its human form. I waited until it was over and he rolled over in a sweaty, naked heap.

I took advantage of his weakness and stood up, forcing

my voice to stay steady as I told him, "I have to go." Then I turned and started running away from him, away from his kisses, away from his embrace. Away from his love.

"Don't you fucking dare," he shouted behind me. "Lis, come back." I'd run far, but not far enough that I didn't hear him say, "Please don't leave me." I stopped running and wrapped my arms around myself, his words almost breaking my resolve. His smell got closer, so I started running again. He chased me through the forest. We were both equally matched, but I couldn't let him catch me.

He was gaining on me, and I picked up speed until I heard him cry out in pain. I faltered, only for a moment, and then he slammed into me, throwing us both to the ground. We plunged down a hill, his arms holding me to protect my head. When we stopped rolling, we lay side by side and he didn't let me go. I thought about fighting him, but I couldn't do it. I brought my hands up to clutch his back.

"Don't leave," he whispered into my hair. "Please don't leave."

"I have to." I hugged him tighter. Just a few more moments by his side. "I can't let them find you. They'll take you to the Lycans."

"They won't find us," he said firmly. "I'll protect you. I promised I'd keep you safe."

I pulled away so I could scowl at his face. He was going to get himself killed because he cared too much about the protection he was obliged to give me. "Forget the promise. Forget the Alpha's bracelet."

"This isn't about a stupid bracelet, you ass." He grabbed my wrists and brought them up in front of me. The bracelet was gone. "Look. You lost it when Arthur took you. If I stay with you, it's because I want to."

"And if I leave you, it's because I want to," I countered. "I abandoned my friends to protect them. If I can protect you by doing so, I will."

"We're beyond this, Lis. If any speck of what we've been through has taught us anything, it's that if we're going to survive, we need each other." He brought a hand up to tuck some hair behind my ear. "Please. Trust that I can protect myself, and you."

Tears welled in my eyes. "I've felt the pain of losing people I loved. It never goes away. You just learn to live with it. And I can't do that with you. I don't know why, but I can't."

He stared at me, his hand still resting on my cheek. "Lis…"

We both stiffened when we heard something in the forest.

I looked back at him in a panic. "They're here." It wasn't just the Hunters I felt. I could sense several Lycan packs coming in from all directions.

We were surrounded.

I saw it in his face when he realized it as well. I reached up and took his hand on my cheek. They would kill him. He'd be gone forever. My knight, my protector. Suddenly the thought of my fate with the Order didn't seem so bad. At least I wouldn't have to live in a world without Knight. A world without sunlight.

A thought entered my head, something I'd been fighting this whole time, but it felt so right, I couldn't help myself. I leaned forward and kissed Knight on his perfect lips. He whimpered as I explored his mouth with my tongue. We only had moments, and I wasn't going to waste them.

Resting my forehead against his, I stroked his cheek and kissed him once, lightly, before looking into his eyes. "I love you." A sob broke from my chest, finally knowing the truth inside me. "I do. I love you."

He didn't even hesitate in his response to my declaration. "Gods, I love you so much, Lis." Another kiss, and another. As many as we could get.

The Lycans and Hunters were closer. In the distance, I could hear the Lycans growling as they got closer. I gasped, grabbing Knight to me. I wasn't scared of Lycans. I was scared because the closer they got, the less time I had with him. He held me tight and combed his fingers through my hair. "I won't let them take you," he whispered to me. I felt tears fall down my cheeks. He knew he couldn't save me, or himself. He was only trying to make me feel better. As he always did.

"Don't lie to me," I told him with a sob. "Don't ever lie to me."

"Please don't cry, Lis," he pleaded softly. "I've seen you cry so many times. But you're so strong. You have to stay strong for me. No matter what happens, promise?" I nodded against his shoulder. He pulled me back for another deep and meaningful kiss before our pursuers reached us. I savored the feel of his lips, his scent in my nose, and even the smell of his blood.

Time stopped around us, and nothing mattered except the feeling of our lips and bodies together. I knew I could kiss him for a hundred years and still always, always would need and want more. More of him. More of us. Every moment together, it had always been him, from that first day when he smiled at me.

I loved him so much. I wanted to cry over the depth of my feelings, because here, on the last moment of my freedom, was the moment I'd found my soul mate. The one I'd been searching for ever since I was a fledgling, and he'd been here this whole time. It didn't matter that he was a werewolf, and he didn't care that I was a vampire. We'd found love in an unexpected source, in the one person we never thought it would happen with. And with the only person we wanted it to happen with.

In that soft little moment, I felt complete. And I was ready to face my fate.

We were still kissing when they got to us.

The first thing they did was hit Knight with a dart. He slumped against me, still conscious but he could barely move. Two large Lycans came up to us, shoved me aside, and picked Knight off the ground. They still had a wary attitude towards him, the unknown element amongst their pack.

"I really wish I was wearing some fucking pants," he said weakly, giving me a slight smile. I wasn't complaining. The only thing I hated was now all of our attackers would see his erection. One of the Hunters grabbed my arm and made me stand. Our two species stood on either side of the little clearing Knight and I had been sitting in. I watched as one of the Lycans helped Knight put on some shorts to cover himself.

"You kissed a fucking Lycan?" the Hunter holding my arm said, clearly ranking that with eating a rotting maggot. "I'd execute you myself for that if I could."

Arthur came up to us and bitchslapped her on the face. *Damn,* he was a cunt. "Your judgment means nothing, Cassandra. As revolting as kissing a Lycan is, it's not against the law."

"It should be," Cassandra whispered in defiance. Arthur gave her a warning look, silently asking if she wanted another slap, as he locked my wrists in irons and chains. Olivier replaced Cassandra on the arm grabbing, except her grip on my bicep wasn't so tight. Knight was still hanging limply between his captors.

"Please don't hurt him," I pleaded with the Alpha of the pack, a blonde rugged man.

The Alpha looked me over, his face displaying a small

amount of the disgust the Hunters were feeling over me kissing a Lycan. "He's a Primal werewolf. It's too dangerous to let him live."

"He's not dangerous," I told the Alpha, pleading for the man I loved. "I watched him. He only attacked to protect himself. Don't kill him just because he's different."

"Enough," Arthur declared sharply. "We've lingered here for too long. The Order is waiting." Arthur reached for the arm Olivier wasn't holding, but she pulled me away.

"Let her say goodbye," she said firmly to Arthur. He sighed and nodded to her with respect. "Be quick," she told me.

Knight lifted his head to look at me and smiled weakly. "Remember your promise, Lis." Stay strong. Stay strong for him.

"I love you." My voice wobbled and I held back the tears that wanted to overwhelm me. I'd never meant anything more in my life. I loved him. I would always love him.

His smile deepened, and he stared at me with love and respect, in honor of everything. The pain, the struggles, the laughter, and the passion. "I love you, Lis."

Arthur stepped forward, grabbed me, and slung me over his shoulder. As he and the Hunters walked in the other direction, my eyes didn't leave Knight's face until I couldn't see him anymore.

I pushed out my senses and focused on him so hard I could feel his mind inside my own. He gasped at the sensation, and when he could catch his breath, he said one thing to me.

"I'll find you again."

I snapped back into my own head and felt my blood reserves fade away as I lost consciousness, taking away the only thing I had left of him.

NOTES

2. POWDERED CONFECTIONS

1. Ma belle mademoiselle: My beautiful miss
2. Ma cherie: My darling
3. Charmante: Charming
4. Mon dieu: My god.

3. BACON, BACON, BACON

1. Mi amore: My love
2. Bon chance: Good luck.

Glossary

*B*icus: A collective term for the sibling creatures known as Incubus and Succubus.

Bonding ceremony: A vampire wedding involving a vow between the couple, exchanging of each other's blood, and mixing their blood together through a cut on their wrists.

Born vampires: The product of an Incubus and human female union. They can turn humans, create drones, and give birth to new vampires. Born vampires must drink fresh human blood every day. Drinking bagged human blood cannot sustain them and will cause them to slowly starve.

Companion: A term for the humans that serve vampires. They sign a ten year contract and are chosen by a vampire to live in their rooms, and be willingly bitten once a day to feed the vampire. Once their contract is up they can either renew it, or they can leave with a promised sum of money upon contract termination.

Council: A group comprised of the heads of each vampire Order. They oversee all vampires, pass judgement for infractions, and direct the vampire Hunters.

Dhampir: The product of a vampire and human union. None were known to exist as the two species typically do not mix romantically.

Frenzy: A state vampires reach when they are so starved

of blood their body can no longer cope. They become wild, their eyes glow red, and they will attack until their hunger is sated.

Hunters: A group comprised solely of Born vampires whose sole purpose is to hunt down any vampire that has broken the law, and either bring them to justice or execute them.

Incubus: A creature of seduction, built for the sole purpose of coupling with female humans to create new Born vampires. If an Incubus falls in love, they develop a distinctive scent.

Lycans: The product of a Primal werewolf and human female union. They can shift into a wolf whenever they like.

Primal werewolves: Originally human men who have been scratched by a succubus, turning them to a werewolf when the full moon rises.

The Bicus plane: A mystical realm only accessible to those with the blood of the Bicus. Time moves differently inside the plane, moving slower or faster than Earth depending on the moment.

The Order Acilino: Location in Spain, "Eagle."

The Order Bête: Location in Canada, "Beast."

The Order Dedliwan: Location in Australia, to "Deadly."

The Order Engel: Location in Greenland, "Angel."

The Order Gennadi: Location in Russia, "Noble."

The Order Janiccat: Location in Malaysia, "Born."

The Order Khalid: Location in Algeria, "Immortal."

The Order Oleander: Location in the United States, "Poisonous."

The Order Qiángdù: Location in China, "Strength."

The Order Raposa: Location in Brazil, "Fox."

The Order Safed: Location in India, "Undamaged."

The Order Sangre: Location in Mexico, name translates to "Blood."

The turned vampires: Vampires that used to be humans and have been. Note: the word "turned" in reference to this type of vampire is never capitalized, hence referring to them as "the turned" to avoid this. They cannot turn humans, or give birth. The turned must drink human blood every day. Unlike the Born vampires, the turned vampires can survive on bagged blood.

Vaewolf: The product of a Primal werewolf or Lycan and a vampire union. They can shift into a wolf whenever they like, they have vampire fangs, and they require blood to heal if they are seriously injured. They do not require daily blood like vampires do.

Vipyre: The product of an Incubus and vampire female union. An incredibly rare creature, only one has ever been known to exist, but it is most likely due to lost knowledge as these creatures have been written about in Incubi lore.

Bathory Family

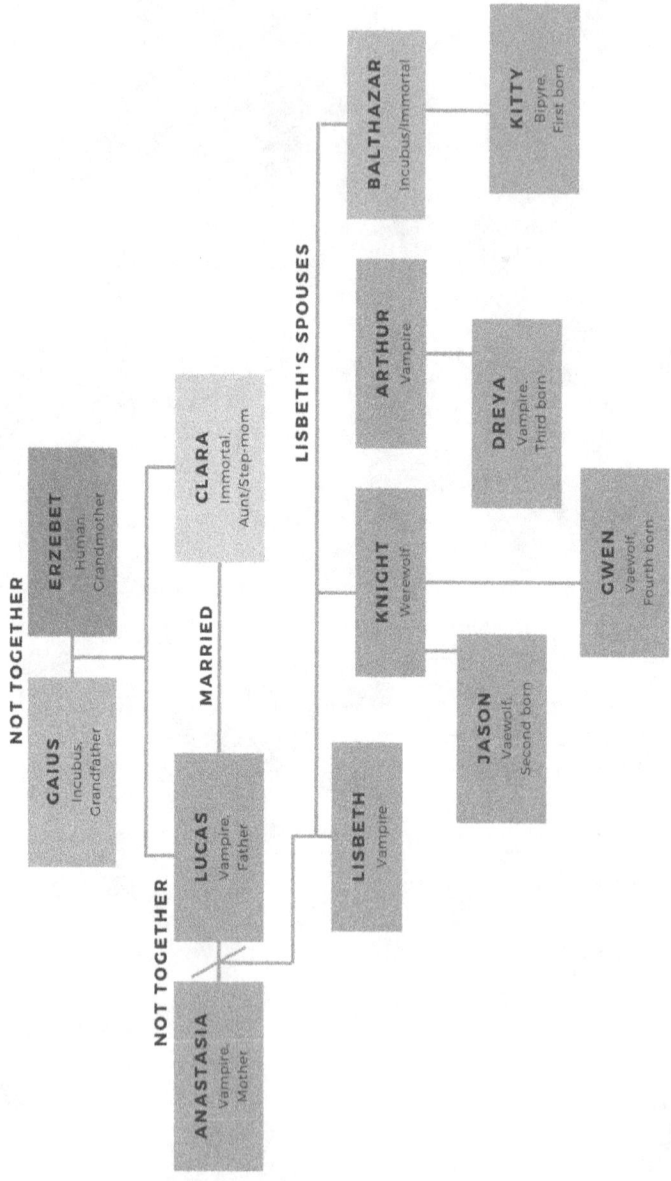

NOT TOGETHER

GAIUS
Incubus,
Grandfather

ERZEBET
Human,
Grandmother

CLARA
Immortal
Aunt/Step-mom

MARRIED

NOT TOGETHER

ANASTASIA
Vampire,
Mother

LUCAS
Vampire,
Father

LISBETH
Vampire

LISBETH'S SPOUSES

JASON
Vaewolf,
Second born

KNIGHT
Werewolf

GWEN
Vaewolf,
Fourth born

ARTHUR
Vampire

DREVA
Vampire,
Third born

BALTHAZAR
Incubus/Immortal

KITTY
Bipyre,
First born

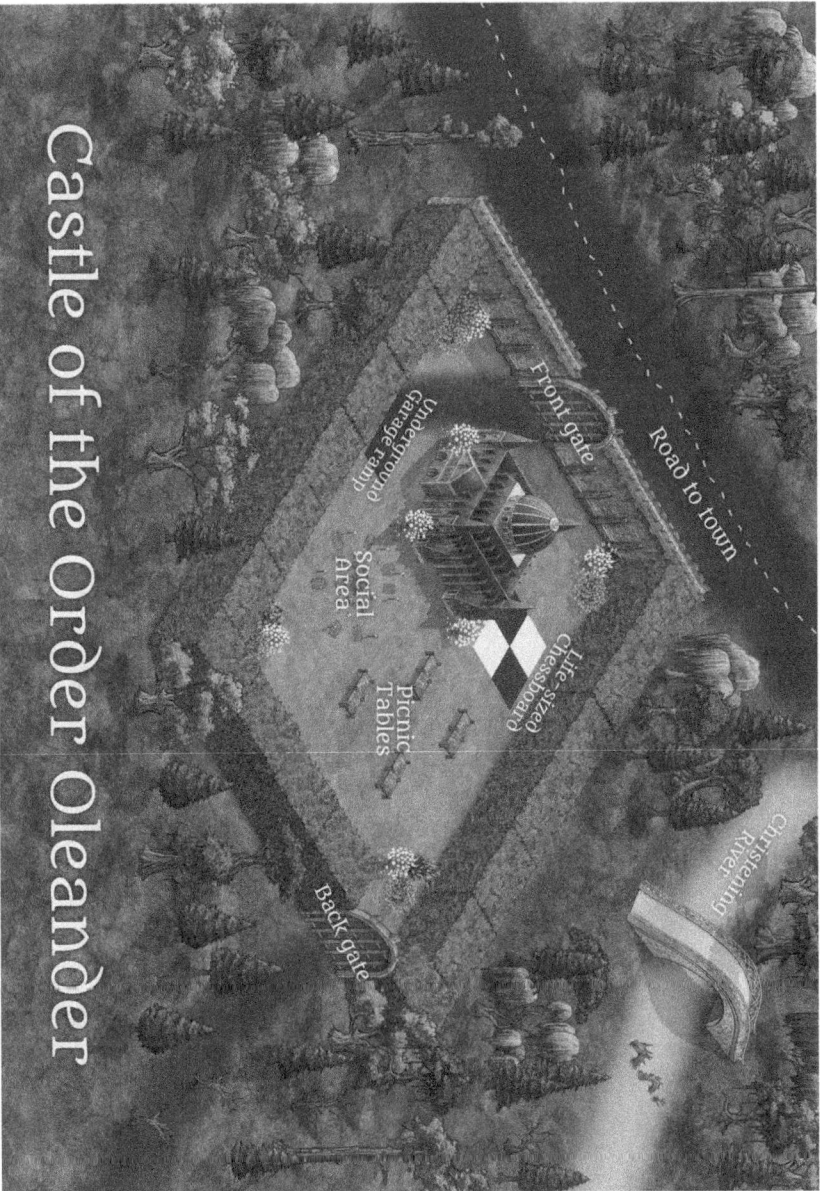

Castle of the Order Oleander

Road to town

Front gate

Underground
Garage ramp

Social
Area

Picnic
Tables

Life-sized
Chessboard

Back gate

Christening
River

ABOUT THE AUTHOR

Photo by Elizabeth Dunlap

Elizabeth Dunlap is the author of several fantasy books, including the Born Vampire series. She's never wanted to be anything else in her life, except maybe a vampire. She lives in Texas with her boyfriend, their daughter, and a very sleepy chihuahua named Deyna.

You can find her online at
www.elizabethdunlap.com

> facebook.com/elizabethdunlapnifty
> twitter.com/edunlapnifty
> instagram.com/edunlapnifty
> goodreads.com/Elizabeth_Dunlap
> bookbub.com/authors/elizabeth-dunlap
> amazon.com/author/ElizabethDunlap

CPSIA information can be obtained
at www.ICGtesting.com
Printed in the USA
LVHW031938251120
672678LV00003BA/460

9 781393 441908